"You're bea...

She raised an eyebrow. "I'm still not entering into some arranged marriage."

"Nobody arranged anything for us. We should both choose this marriage because it's the right thing to do. It is the only honorable course of action. My country and my people expect no less from me."

"Marrying for protocol's sake? Living some happy royal farce for the media?"

Her face had been on his mind every day since she'd left him. Her body—sans clothes—had been a major player in his dreams.

"If I married for protocol, according to the wishes of the Council, I would marry for alliance. I would marry a princess for her father's wealth and influence," he informed her.

"Sounds good to me. You should try and keep this Council happy. They sound important."

"They'll be happy that I finally secured an heir. This might not be the marriage they had in mind, but they won't protest it."

"*I* protest it. I'm not entering into a fake marriage so you can parade my son around as your heir."

"Nothing about our marriage would be fake, I promise you that, Isabelle," he told her before he kissed her.

DANA MARTON

THE BLACK SHEEP SHEIK

TORONTO NEW YORK LONDON
AMSTERDAM PARIS SYDNEY HAMBURG
STOCKHOLM ATHENS TOKYO MILAN MADRID
PRAGUE WARSAW BUDAPEST AUCKLAND

With many thanks to Allison Lyons and Cindy Whitesel.

Special thanks and acknowledgment to Dana Marton for her contribution to the Cowboys Royale series.

Recycling programs
for this product may
not exist in your area.

ISBN-13: 978-0-373-69566-9

THE BLACK SHEEP SHEIK

www.Harlequin.com

Printed in U.S.A.

ABOUT THE AUTHOR

Dana Marton is the author of more than a dozen fast-paced, action-adventure romantic suspense novels and a winner of the Daphne du Maurier Award of Excellence. She loves writing books of international intrigue, filled with dangerous plots that try her tough-as-nails heroes and the special women they fall in love with. Her books have been published in seven languages in eleven countries around the world. When not writing or reading, she loves to browse antiques shops and enjoys working in her sizable flower garden, where she searches for "bad" bugs with the skills of a superspy and vanquishes them with the agility of a commando soldier. Every day in her garden is a thriller. To find more information on her books, please visit www.danamarton.com. She loves to hear from her readers and can be reached via email at DanaMarton@DanaMarton.com.

Books by Dana Marton

HARLEQUIN INTRIGUE

*Mission: Redemption
**Defending the Crown

CAST OF CHARACTERS

Amir Khalid—The black sheep sheik of Jamala has just taken on the burden of ruling his country and isn't looking for additional commitments. But when he finds out that the American woman he could never forget is carrying his child, he needs every weapon at his disposal to convince her to commit to him.

Isabelle Andrews—The stubborn sheik of Jamala who won't take no for an answer becomes the least of the beautiful doctor's problems when she's kidnapped just as she's about to go into labor.

Darek, Prince of Saruk—His father had been an enemy to Amir, but Darek wants friendship. Or does he?

Jake Wolfe—Sheriff of Wind River County. Although the previous administration had been corrupt, Jake Wolfe seems firmly on the royals' side. At least Amir hopes he is, since Jake is set on marrying his sister.

Sheik Efraim—Amir's best friend. He's frantic with worry when Amir goes missing, then rushes to the rescue when he's needed.

Chapter One

He looked up at the wood beams of the rustic cabin's ceiling and, for one bewildering moment, couldn't remember anything. He didn't know how he'd come to be there, in the out-of-place hospital bed, hooked up to machines. He didn't even know his own name.

All he knew was that he was in danger. And choking.

He yanked out the tubes that obstructed his airway and drew a ragged breath. As he breathed, in great heaving gulps, everything rushed back in a dizzying flood of information. A car explosion. Fire. Somebody trying to kill him.

Then a name: *Amir Khalid.*

He was Sheik Amir of Jamala, ruler of a small Mediterranean island nation. But this wasn't home, far from it. He was in Wyoming for a business summit and to find the American doctor who, for months now, had haunted his dreams.

He squinted against the late-afternoon sun that streamed in through the windows, still plenty hot in the middle of summer. Nothing but open land out there and a stand of trees in the distance. If he'd been rescued from the explosion, he would be in a hospital. That he was in the middle of nowhere could mean only one thing.

Kidnapped.

A car door slammed outside.

He tugged off the medical attachments from his chest and arm, then sat up, a wave of dizziness hitting him. He held on to the edge of the bed. Anger swept through him, his hands fisting at the thought of being incapacitated and at the mercy of his enemies.

Get going. Get out.

He put his feet to the floor and pushed to standing, but his legs couldn't remember how to walk. His knees buckled.

Move. Escape.

He swallowed the bitterness bubbling up his throat. Not that long ago, his first thought wouldn't have been running. It would have been confronting his enemies, defeating them or going out in a blaze of glory. Now his first priority had to be his safety. The fate of a whole country depended on him; the lives of millions were in his hands. He had to let his security force handle the bastards who had put him in this shape, no matter how much beating a retreat went against his grain.

He needed to switch his hospital gown for real clothes, find a cell phone and a weapon—not necessarily in that order. The one-bedroom cabin held a sofa bed and his hospital bed in the living area, kitchen cabinets lining the far wall, the pots and pans on the shelf interspersed with old golf trophies. Nothing beyond the basic necessities, not even a TV. He noted the two doors, one to the outside, closed, one to a small bathroom, open.

Keep moving.

He dragged himself over to the kitchen counter, leaning against the wall the whole way. His joints had rusted up; his muscles felt as if they'd gone on vacation. His mind was foggy; his thoughts disjointed. Maybe the explosion had given him a concussion. Frustration filled him to the brim, but was pierced by a ray of hope when he spotted the knife in the sink.

He grabbed the meager weapon, then stumbled toward the pegs on the wall by the front door, aiming for the worn rain slicker to cover the hospital gown he was wearing. He had almost reached it when the door opened—the blinding sunlight outlining a dark shape.

Head down, he put whatever strength he had into slamming the bastard into the wall and braced for pain. But instead of an eruption of violence, he nearly folded to the floor. Slim arms reached out to hold him up.

"You shouldn't be out of bed."

He looked up into blue eyes that were filled with concern and some other, harder emotion, a familiar face framed with long black hair. A new wave of confusion washed over him. "Isabelle?"

Maybe his concussion was more severe than he'd thought. Maybe he was hallucinating. But no, the woman in front of him was all too real. She took the knife from him as easily as if from a child, tossed it onto the counter and tried to help him back to the hospital bed.

His masculine pride insisted on the sofa, and so did he.

"Okay. For a little while," said that sensuous voice he hadn't been able to forget. "How do you feel?"

The same way he'd felt when he'd been thrown by the lead camel at a race a couple of years ago and stomped on by the rest. He wasn't about to tell her that, not until he got his bearings and figured out what was going on. His voice was rough and rusty as he asked the most basic question, "Where are we?"

"At my father's hunting cabin. He used to call it his escape pod. I don't think he actually ever hunted. He came here to avoid my mother." She talked to him slowly, in a reassuring tone, a doctor who knew she had a disoriented patient on her hands.

Yet there was some tightness around her eyes— anger?—that put him on guard. Just because he remembered her most fondly, it didn't mean she felt the same, although he couldn't think of why she would be mad at him.

Yet her posture was rigid. "How is your throat?"

He swallowed painfully. "Raw."

A slight breeze blew in through the open door. He turned his face into it for a second and figured out at last why the air smelled all wrong in this place. He couldn't smell the ocean.

He wanted to ask why they were here, but he registered her full body at last, his mind beginning to function a little better, the mental haze thinning. He blinked hard. "You're pregnant." His voice sounded even hoarser than before.

"Why, thank you for noticing," she said with a dose of sarcasm as she stepped away from him, moving briskly to the hospital bed to shut off the machines, then to the door to close it.

"Are we safe?"

"Nobody knows you're here."

He didn't feel safe. His instincts still signaled danger.

Everything around him was small, the cabin all wood and unfamiliar. His country being an island nation, they didn't have an overabundance of trees. Buildings were made of stone or brick, which kept their interior cool during the hot Mediterranean summers. He felt out of place here.

"I need my phone."

"Absolutely not." She had her strict doctor face on as she came back to him. "Whatever business you have can wait. First things first."

She reached for the old-fashioned blood-pressure cuff on the coffee table and wrapped it around his arm and started to pump it. Her long, slim fingers woke up nerve endings wherever she touched him.

"You shouldn't even be out of bed. Stay off your feet. Your blood pressure could drop without notice. You don't want to fall and bang yourself up all over again."

He needed to talk to her about the danger they were in, but his gaze kept slipping to her round belly. Disappointment and some other stronger emotion, one he didn't care to examine, filled up his chest. "You are married?"

"In this day and age, a woman doesn't need a husband to have a baby." She had a scowl on her face as she lifted a finger so he'd stay quiet while she counted. "Blood pressure's a little low, but not bad, all things considered." She put the cuff away, then left him again to go to the kitchen.

He wished she would stay put by his side for a while to give him a chance to drink in the sight of her, a chance to sort his thoughts into some order. Against her medical advice, he tried to rise, but his legs wouldn't support him, so he slumped back onto the sofa with ill grace.

"Who?" He wanted to know who had seduced her, then abandoned her, so he could have some words with the blackguard as soon as he felt better. The thought of anyone hurting Isabelle was intolerable. "What's his name?"

She was searching for something in the refrigerator, ignoring him. She was just as beautiful as he remembered, her movements graceful despite her swollen belly, her eyes intelligent and inquisitive.

Despite the months that had passed since their first and only meeting, his attraction hadn't lessened any.

"Want to tell me who wants you dead?" She put a pot of something on the electric stove, studiously keeping her eyes on the task, almost as if wanting to avoid his gaze.

"The million-dollar question." He sounded every bit as morose as he felt. His memory had big, gaping holes in it. "What happened last night? I don't remember everything."

He didn't remember when she'd come into the picture, or how he'd gotten here. He clamped his teeth, hating to admit weakness, hating to be sitting there, disoriented, clad only in a hospital gown— not exactly the image he'd planned to project when he'd decided to find the American doctor he'd had a two-day affair with, then couldn't forget.

"Let's see." She looked at him as she stirred the pot, and watched him carefully. "Last night I tried to catch up on my medical journals. You were in a coma. Same old, same old."

His mind, barely settled since he'd woken, went into another spin. "A coma? For more than a day?" Had the summit started without him? He was one of five royals, all leading small Mediterranean island nations, who'd come to the United States for trade negotiations and agreements about undersea oil fields. The economic recovery of other countries depended on this summit, not just his.

Pity suffused her delicate face. "A month. Take it easy, all right? You'll be fine. You made it. Don't stress yourself out. You need to keep calm and you need to be resting."

The cabin closed in around him, all that dark wood making him feel like he was trapped in a cave. He wanted the spacious rooms of his palace with their whitewashed walls and tall ceilings, with all those open views of the Mediterranean Sea surrounding his island. He wanted normal and familiar, a point of reference. His ears were buzzing.

"How?" The one-word question tore from his throat.

"Your limousine blew up on the road I usually take to work. I was driving to the hospital in Dumont for my shift, and there you were, trying to climb from the wreckage. I recognized you. You asked for my help. You demanded that I not call the authorities."

He recalled the phone threat Prince Stefan had received the day they had arrived in the United States, the threatening letters he himself had received in the leading up to their trip. He also remembered now that minute or two after the explosion, mangled thoughts mixed in with the pain.

He had thought he would just need a minute to recover. Then he could go back to the resort, and between him and his friends they would figure out what was going on, figure out the publicity angle. He had wanted his security to check the scene before the police cordoned off the area as their crime scene.

His next thought made his stomach clench with dread. "The driver?"

Her lips flattened into a grim line. "Dead on impact. You had minor burns and some serious lacerations. Hit your head pretty hard. All in all, you were very lucky."

He hung his head, not feeling lucky in the least. He would have Bahur's family found and would make sure they were taken care of. The least he could do was to make sure that they had everything they needed. Guilt ate at him as he thought of the years the man had spent in his service, the future Bahur had been robbed of.

Because of him.

Those threatening notes hadn't been bluffing. They weren't some discontent coward's way of trying to spread fear, as he had first hoped. His enemies *were* prepared to kill.

And here he was, in the middle of nowhere, unarmed and without any security. With Isabelle. Which made a bad situation intolerable. "My presence here puts you in danger."

"Nobody knows."

Except, an enemy who was resourceful enough to gain details of his top-secret trip to the United States, and could get close enough to put a bomb in his limousine, obviously had considerable resources and investigative skills. "We will leave this place. Thank you for bringing me here and hiding me," he added, wanting to make sure that she knew her help was appreciated.

For a moment she looked unsettled, as if not quite sure what to do with him. "You were in and out of it at first, pretty adamant that I shouldn't call anyone. Then you lost it completely, and I was dialing 9-1-1 when this shady-looking guy came to the door, pretending to be an investigator, asking if I saw the explosion, if I saw anyone driving by or walking away from the wreckage. He had an accent."

"What kind?"

"A hard accent. Not French, for sure. Russian, maybe." She paused for a second. "His hand kept straying to his back. I was pretty sure he had a gun ready. He gave me the creeps. I hung up the phone. Later that night I brought you out here. I was going to call an ambulance if your condition took a turn for the worse, if your vitals became unstable. They never did." Her voice was soft, but that tightness still lingered around her eyes.

Her attitude toward him seemed to be a mixture of concern and resentment. Yet, somehow he got the feeling that the resentment wasn't about the imposition of her having to take care of him.

"You saved my life." No question about that. The kingdom of Jamala and he, personally, owed her a great debt. She and her child would be taken care of and would never have to feel the sting of the father's abandonment. "I owe you my gratitude."

She shrugged that off. "You had the good sense to be in a light coma. Any worse and I wouldn't have had a choice but to take you in for intensive care. And you get points for getting blown up with a doctor in hailing distance."

He'd been in high spirits that night, just back from an evening in town with his friends. Their first day in the United States. And he couldn't let it end without seeing Isabelle. "I was coming back to you. I should have come sooner."

She busied herself with stirring the soup. "It doesn't matter."

But it did. Because if he had come back months ago, hadn't let her slip away after their amazing weekend, then she wouldn't have met another man, wouldn't be carrying another man's child now. Had he expected that after all this time she would wait for him? A part of him, deep down, obviously had.

Something sharp stabbed him in the middle of his chest.

He had meant to come back, had made plans. But matters of the state had interfered. He was a sheik; his time was not his own. Not even now.

"Have you heard anything about the royals at the Wind River Ranch and Resort?" He needed to call Stefan, Efraim and the others. They were probably searching for him. His disappearance must have messed up the negotiations between the United States and their Coalition of Island Nations, COIN.

She put the soup on the table, looking at home in the small kitchen. "All over the news, according to the nurses. They can't even stop talking about it when I call into the hospital to check in on the patients I had to hand off because of the maternity leave. It's been like the Wild West returned over at the resort with all those princes. Never a dull moment, apparently."

His muscles clenched. "Has anyone been harmed?" Those four men were like brothers to him, even closer to his heart than his recently found half brother, Wade, who was yet another reason for his being in Wyoming. A quest that would now have to wait.

"Someone was shot, but not one of the royals."

A confused second passed before he remembered that she didn't know his true identity. Their two passionate days together had been pure fantasy, strangers acting out a scene from the tales of the Thousand and One Nights. And now…with danger all around and him as weak as he was…probably not the best time to tell her. He needed to regain his strength and orient himself much better before he trusted anyone.

"We eat, and then we leave," was all he told her. He needed to know for certain who his friends were and who his enemies were.

The phone threat texted to Stefan and the letters to him had to be connected. He'd received those letters back in Jamala. And Stefan received the text message before they even landed here. His instincts said whomever was behind the threats was from the islands and was not an American.

The miserable old king of Saruk came to mind, head of a larger neighboring country that wanted all the undersea oil rights, among other things.

Five years ago he would have been the first person Amir would have looked at. But Prince Darek was taking over more and more of his father's duties, making most, if not all, of the important decisions, and Darek was a good man, a friend. Amir trusted him.

So where did the threat originate? He had opponents back at home, of course. The summit had opponents, too. He cracked his knuckles. Either way, his enemy was either here now or used American accomplices. Someone had put a bomb on that limousine.

"Food is ready." Isabelle was putting plates on the table, a picture of domestic femininity even with that tension he didn't understand still in her shoulders. "You stay put. I'll bring you a tray."

He pushed to his feet, succeeding this time. "I'll never regain my strength if all I do is sit around."

And he needed his strength back desperately. Whoever had sent those threatening notes had taken things to the next level with the bomb in the car. He'd made his first kill, even if the driver had been an unintended victim. But the attacker was clearly committed to his goal, set on his course. He wasn't going to give up until he accomplished whatever he was after.

His friends and he were in danger. And Isabelle was in danger by simply being with him. That last bit bothered him the most. She had nothing to do with politics. Her only crime was saving him.

But he would protect her with his life, if needed. "We should hurry."

He pushed forward, his progress embarrassingly slow, a contrast to his words. When he made it to the table, he sank onto the chair with relief. He watched with appreciation as she ladled rich vegetable soup onto his plate. The aroma filled the one-room cabin, instantly making the strange place seem more welcoming.

He had pictured their reunion a dozen times in the past few months, but never under these circumstances. She sat across the table from him, unable to pull up her chair all the way due to her swollen belly. Her skin glowed; her black hair was lustrous and shiny. Pregnancy became her. He couldn't say he had contemplated pregnant women all that much in the past, but she was both desirable and fascinating.

"Since you've been here, taking care of me all this time, I'm guessing the father of the baby is no longer in the picture."

He had mixed feelings about that. Outrage that the bastard had abandoned her, and relief that he didn't have to see her with another man, the thought of which was enough to make him clench his teeth and fist his hands on the table. There was a part of him that had thought of her all these months as his.

Sheer idiocy. Of course others wanted her, courted her. The thought was like a thousand daggers cutting his skin.

She opened a bag of bread, pulled the butter away

from him. Avoided his gaze. "You should eat light for the next couple of days. Your stomach hasn't seen solid food in a while."

"Do you not want to talk to me about the father? The shame is his for abandoning his responsibilities, not yours." He shook his head. "American men these days, they grow up on television and video games, having too much, without a real man's sense of what duty is."

But he was here now. As soon as their stomachs were filled, he was going to take her to safety. He was going to protect her and her unborn baby.

"American men are fine." She drew a slow breath, no longer bothering to disguise the anger and resentment in her tone. "You're the father, okay?"

Chapter Two

Somewhere in the city of Dumont, Wyoming, a telephone rang in a dark, abandoned warehouse, the sound bouncing off the empty walls and filling the space. Long seconds ticked by before anyone responded.

"I think we know where he is," the caller said when the line was finally picked up.

"Do we have confirmation?"

"Not yet."

"How soon?"

"Within the hour."

"Get the men ready."

"Yes, sir."

"No more mistakes."

"No, sir. Should we bring him to you when we have him?"

"Yes, but not here. I'll be changing locations. I'll call you from the new place and give directions when I get there."

"Yes, sir. And if he has anyone with him?"

A moment of silence, then, "You know who I want. Everyone else is expendable."

The line went dead as the call ended.

ISABELLE WATCHED AMIR from under hooded eyelids. Yep, she should have definitely waited with her big surprise.

He'd just come out of a coma. He should still be in bed. Not that she would ever be able to get him back in there now. He had stubborn written all over him. He had walked to the table, for heaven's sake. He seemed determined to pretend that there was nothing wrong with him. Men and their foolish pride. Someone needed to invent a pill for that. If only.

"You need rest. We can talk about this later." *Or not at all.* "You need to get back to your family and a physical therapist who can help you regain your strength. I have to get back home and get ready for the baby's birth."

She had a week left, at most. If he hadn't awakened in a day or two, she would have had to make the difficult decision of what to do with him. She could no longer stay with him at the cabin, and she couldn't have left him here alone, either, not without medical assistance.

Yes, she was mad at him for manipulating her the night they first met, but she was a doctor. She would never be mad enough at anyone to provide less than the best medical assistance she was capable of. Not even if the lying weasel bastard had tricked her into his bed and left her pregnant.

The worst part was that after all that, she was *still* attracted to him. She had to be stupider than shipping peanuts. Seriously. Any other woman would have strangled the man by now. Not her, she'd carefully taken care of him.

His tumultuous dark gaze was fixed on her belly, his gaze like a physical touch on her skin. "Are you certain about paternity?"

Oh, that was rich. He was questioning *her* word? She bit her lower lip, then let it go, pulled her aching spine straight. "I am. And I'm not going to be offended by the question, because you don't really know me, but this is the only pass you're going to get on the subject."

He raised his gaze to her, sharp now like a hawk's. His shoulders tensed. His voice was cold as he asked, "What do you want from me?"

She shouldn't have been disappointed. This was exactly what she'd expected in the unlikely case that the prince of Persia ever returned.

"How about your name, for starters?" After evading the truth so skillfully when they'd first met, now that the question was put to him straight, would he lie about his identity?

Nine months ago they'd met at the hospital's annual charity ball, a masquerade. She'd been Isabelle the Harem Flower. All six of the women from general surgery were decked out to the nines in belly-dancing outfits—Janie's idea since she'd been taking lessons to revive her marriage.

He'd worn the costume of a Persian prince to the charity ball, a flowing, colorful robe. His midnight eyes called her from across the room. He'd walked straight to her without noticing any of the women who gaped at him. They'd discussed health care, of all things, which still needed improvement in his home country, Jamala, he'd told her in the most charming accent. His intelligence had seduced her as much as his rich voice and the way his dark gaze drank her in.

She had no idea how she'd ended up in his suite at the Wind River Ranch and Resort, but she knew with absolute certainty that it wouldn't have happened if she'd known that he was a sheik! Yep, he'd skipped that little detail.

She'd stayed with him for two whole days, doing little more than making love and ordering room service. She'd left without waking him, nearly late for her emergency O.R. shift, at 2:00 a.m. on the third day, still thinking him some foreign hospital administrator here to do benchmarking or whatever.

"So no name, huh?" Resentment welled inside her for having been duped so thoroughly. "It would be nice to know what to say once the kid starts asking."

She'd been too embarrassed to go back to him once she'd gotten off work. She'd never lost control like that before. She barely even dated, let alone had passionate affairs with strangers. Med school, residency, then her insane surgery schedule left her neither time nor energy for men. Having a serious relationship was on her to-do list, just scheduled for a much later date. After she'd made chief of surgery, maybe.

By the time she'd figured out that she was pregnant, he had checked out, and the resort, of course, would divulge no information on the mysterious guest in the Emerald Suite.

But here he was now, even if with his amazing lips pressed in a thin line, he didn't look like he was keen on her giving any more information than he'd given her before, which was pretty much nothing.

She tilted her head, incredulity creeping into her voice as she asked, "I can't know your name?" Her fingers itched to grab him by the shoulders and shake him. Not that she would ever do that to a patient.

A tense couple of seconds passed. His gaze slipped to her belly, then slowly returned to her face.

"Amir Khalid." He stood and gave a small but formal bow, watching her as if he could see right inside of her, to her deepest, darkest secrets.

"Isabelle Andrews." Of course, he probably knew that if he knew where she lived. He'd said he was coming to see her the night he'd gotten injured. So he'd investigated her. She wasn't sure how that made her feel.

"Sheik Amir Khalid," he said, adding his title, then waited a beat. "You don't seem surprised. You knew my name already."

She held his gaze without blinking. "Your friends at the resort made a rather passionate plea on television for information on your whereabouts. Your picture was all over the news."

His face turned grim. "I regret that I involved you in this. I'm afraid that by coming to you, I might have put you in jeopardy."

"Nobody knows. Relax. I didn't even call your friends. There were some news reports on a possible conspiracy or whatever that went as far as the local cops. I didn't know who to trust."

"My friends you can trust."

"How about you? Can I trust you?"

He looked taken aback. "We should leave here as soon as we can. Of course you can trust me."

Not a chance. "But you never trusted me." She pointed out. "If you trusted me, you wouldn't have lied about who you were."

"I didn't lie."

"You didn't tell me you were a *sheik*. The Black Sheep Sheik of Jamala. That's what they called you on the news, you know that? Imagine how stupid I felt when I heard it and recognized your picture. What exactly did you do to get that nickname, anyway?"

His eyes narrowed. "I didn't plan for things to happen this way."

Oh, she believed that. "You just planned to make some poor, ordinary woman your entertainment for the weekend. Rich royal sweeps in, seduces clueless chick, goes home and forgets her. Did I hit all the major bullet points?"

"I never forgot." His voice was low; his gaze piercing; his color rising.

Dammit. She drew a slow breath, catching herself too late. She wasn't supposed to get him upset and get his blood pressure up. She was a doctor, for heaven's sake. She'd promised herself that she wasn't going to attack him at first chance.

"How fast can you be ready to move?" he asked.

Again with his insistence that they weren't safe. Thing was, she felt safer here than at just about anyplace else. The cabin had served them well for the last month. She had some medical equipment and meds here, if he relapsed and needed anything. If he really was in as much trouble as he thought he was, then going to ground made more sense than running around out there. At least until he made a full recovery.

"We'll talk about leaving after you finish your food and put your feet up for a few minutes. How about that? You're no good to anyone if you push yourself too hard and relapse."

He went back to his food, his dark brows furrowed. "Do you still work at the hospital?"

"I took the last month of pregnancy as maternity leave. Can't do those triple shifts. Can't really stand hours on end in the O.R., either." There, that almost came out normal, as if she wasn't spitting mad at him.

"Is everything well with you? With the pregnancy?" His tone was detached.

She made hers match it as she said, "Yes."

Silence stretched between them. She closed her eyes for a second, consoling herself with the fact that the situation couldn't possibly get any worse. Then it did.

"I used protection. I always do." That same emotionless tone again. He was questioning her word.

She hated that. She was a respected surgeon. People normally didn't accuse her of lying, not even in a roundabout way.

"I said one pass." Each word was frostier than the one before. "We slept together nine months ago. I'm nine-months pregnant. Do the math. I haven't been with anybody else since." Or before, really, not for a long time.

Something flashed across his dark gaze but was gone too quickly for her to identify it. He read her much better, apparently, and could see that she was telling the truth, because he magnanimously said, "I believe you." Then ruined the whole effect by adding, "Of course, there'll be a test of paternity."

"I don't want anything from you. I can support this child. He'll be well loved and well taken care of. You can go back home as soon as you recover."

She'd been preparing herself for a future just like that. She didn't need a man in her life. She didn't *want* a man in her life. Another woman might have built up a number of crazy fantasies over the past weeks about him recovering and the two of them riding off into the sunset. She had no illusions. She'd known from early childhood that the whole *happy-American-family* thing was a sham, a marketing message companies used to sell things.

His spoon had stopped halfway to his mouth. "A son?"

"According to the last ultrasound." Despite the strained circumstances of the moment, a thrill ran through her. She couldn't wait to meet her son. She hadn't planned on having a baby just now, all alone, but the thought of that baby made her feel happier than she'd ever been. The two of them were going to make an amazing family.

"A boy for certain?"

She focused back on Amir. "This is not something you have to worry about. My son and I will be fine. I have a whole support system ready. I have great friends. And if you don't believe me about him being yours, that's okay, too. I'm all right with this. I had time to figure it all out. You obviously have your own very serious issues to deal with."

Like the fact that somebody wanted him dead. Her heart twisted at the thought of anyone harming him. They shared a child. Whether they ever saw each other again after this or not, there was a connection between them that would never go away. She couldn't say that the concept didn't make her feel uneasy.

"Tests will be necessary," he continued thoughtfully, "so my son's legitimacy cannot be challenged when the time comes for him to take the throne. He'll be the crown prince. My heir."

"No." Denial flew from her lips as she gripped the edge of the table, pushing her chair back. "Are you kidding me?"

She'd been thinking of her son as hers, singularly hers. She didn't want anyone to have any claim on him, let alone someone as powerful as a sheik. Her son would have a future as a normal little boy, not crippled by expectations and responsibility in some strange, distant country. "That's not necessary. As soon as you're well, you can go back home. You don't need to be involved in this."

"As soon as I'm well, we're getting married." The somber look on his face said he wasn't kidding. Nor was he happy.

Welcome to the club. Maybe they could have T-shirts made and have membership cards printed.

She'd spent the last nine months planning on how she was going to be the best single mom ever. Her plans did *not,* whatsoever, include being married to a sheik.

The sounds of a chopper came through the open windows, coming from the east.

Amir immediately tensed and set his spoon down. "We'll pack and leave now. No hideout is secure if used too long. My enemies had a whole month to track me here."

"This is Wyoming, not the Middle East." Honestly, they were at her father's cabin, in the middle of nowhere. Even some of the locals couldn't find their way out here.

They had the Wind River Mountains to the west and nothing but the Rattlesnake Badlands on the other side as far as the eye could see. Beyond a couple of farmers way down the road, few people lived out this way.

She went to the window to look up at the sky. Amir limped over to pull her back, but she resisted until she got a good look. Did the chopper slow as it flew over them? She couldn't tell for sure, but soon it moved on toward the badlands. "Probably one of the charter tours. They take tourists to see the antelope and the wild mustangs."

He didn't look convinced, didn't relax until he tugged her back to the table. "It might be too late to leave. I shall summon my security here. When they arrive—"

"You're welcome to go with them."

"When you're my wife—"

"Let's make one thing clear," she said as unequivocally as she could. "I'm not marrying you. And I'm not in any kind of danger. You can't use that as an excuse to wrap me in cotton and lock me away. I'm not going to be any man's emotional slave. And I'm not going to be any powerful guy's power play. I'm not going to be your prisoner, with you holding this baby over me."

She clamped her mouth shut, regretting most of that monologue as soon as the last word was out. A simple no would have sufficed. She was projecting and she knew it. But at least she didn't leave any doubt about how she felt. Considering how used to getting his way he must be, that couldn't be a bad thing.

His face hardened on cue, his eyes filling with determination as he took her hands and kept them. "My purpose is not capturing you for selfish reasons. I want only what is best for you and my son. I would give my life to keep you from danger."

The I-control-you-for-your-own-good song and dance. She knew that one by heart, had watched her mother live it with various men after she'd abandoned the family.

"I'm not marrying you, and you can't make me," she told the sheik and she meant it.

He glared regally.

He was the only man she knew who could look magnificent in a hospital gown and make her head swim. Figured. Somehow he managed to radiate strength—along with massive disapproval—even in his current, weakened state.

She hadn't forgotten him in the past nine months, and she was pretty sure she wouldn't have forgotten him—even if he hadn't returned—for as long as she lived. But he did return. She'd been moonstruck enough so that if he'd suggested a loose liaison after the baby was born, she might have gone for it. He was the perfect man to have an affair with.

But what he wanted was to control her completely.

"You carry my son," he said with the arrogance of a man who knew he held the trump card.

"And this is not the Middle Ages," she told him with the certainty of a woman who believed she had sanity and progress on her side. She pulled her hands out of his, at last, away from his tingling heat.

His voice dropped an octave as he said, "Do you hate me that much for not coming back sooner? I did not abandon you. You were gone when I woke. Matters of the state… I had to return home to take care of things."

"I hate you?" She threw her hands up, her frustration escaping at last. She didn't have as good a grip on her emotions these days as she would have liked. A flood of hormones ruled her mind and body.

"Right. I hate you. That's why I put my entire career and everything I worked so hard for at risk by hiding a patient. If anyone found you, I could have lost my medical license. I could have gone to jail."

She'd had plenty of time to worry about that while he'd been out cold. Giving birth in jail wasn't on the list of things she wanted to try. She had risked *everything,* because she couldn't do otherwise. Because she'd believed him when he'd said he was in danger.

His eyes never left her face. "I do thank you for keeping me here all this time. Ask for any reward and I will see that you shall receive it. But the matter of my heir is nonnegotiable."

Of all the magnanimous... She walked away before she could have said something she would regret. "I think I preferred you in a coma. You're much nicer when you're not talking, you know that?"

The prince of Persia she remembered was passionate and...well, *very* passionate and intelligent and had a sense of humor. Also, um, passionate. She swallowed. Sheik Amir Khalid was arranging her life without any regard to her wishes. Nobody was the boss of her. She'd worked hard to make sure that her choices would be her own, that she wouldn't owe anyone anything, that she wouldn't depend on anyone for anything. Ever. She would never be like her mother.

She needed to get out of the cabin and away from him for a while. She had the perfect excuse. "Why don't you lie down and get some rest, give your mind a little time to settle? I need to leave for an hour or two. I have a doctor's appointment today."

"Is something wrong?"

"A regular, scheduled checkup."

Relief crossed his face as he returned to his food. She could see that swallowing was difficult for him, but he was determined to finish. He understood that eating was necessary to regain his strength. Good. At least they wouldn't have to fight about that, because she was about out of the patience she kept in reserve for stubborn sheiks.

"You will not go," he decreed between two

spoonfuls. "I will have the royal physician flown in by tomorrow. He shall take over your care."

She could feel her blood pressure inch up. "I will go to the doctor of my choice. Because I'm a free woman in a free country, and not one of your subjects." She folded her arms over her chest, working hard not to say anything she might regret later. He *was* the father of her child, and he would be that forever. She needed to keep that in mind. Establishing an acrimonious relationship wouldn't serve anyone's interest.

"I am your future husband. You should not think angry thoughts about me," he said with disapproval.

He didn't know half of her angry thoughts. She was happy to fill him in. "I'm thinking whether I'd lose my medical license if I strangled you with the IV line, Your Highness."

She expected him to issue some further royal command, or even a threat, and was ready with a retort. She wasn't scared of him—he'd be lucky if he made it back to the sofa on his own. But instead of berating her for her latest insolence, he laughed. The same laugh that she remembered, the one that had a way of sneaking inside her chest. It completely disarmed her.

The warm, rich sound brought back memories of a luxurious suite with an equally luxurious bed, a thorough seduction, the most amazing two days of her life. The images flitting through her head stole her breath. She turned and busied herself with tidying up his hospital bed while she regained her equilibrium, resenting that he could make her lose it so easily.

He finished his meal and did stagger back to the sofa unaided, abandoning his empty bowl on the table. Of course, His Highness would. She shot him a glare and went to take care of that. She always did all the dishes immediately and kept all food sealed away. Otherwise, she'd have a battle with ants on her hands. Not something on the sheik of Jamala's radar, obviously. He had a palace full of staff to worry about that sort of thing.

"I do need my cell phone now." Sitting with his back supported, he lifted his left leg and tried to hold it steady before lowering it again, then did the same with the right leg.

"You don't have a cell phone. You didn't have much on you when you climbed from the wreckage."

His face turned somber at the mention of the explosion. "Then I'll need yours, if I may."

She pulled it from her pocket and tossed it to him. He caught it. At least his reflexes were okay. He was doing amazingly well, considering that he'd been in a coma for nearly four weeks. His bearing was still regal, his head held high and proud. He could be just as well sitting on a throne than on her worn-out couch. Okay, minus the leg lifts.

"If you don't know who blew up that limo… How do you know whom to trust?" She'd kept him alive this long, and he'd made it. Calling the wrong person could end all that. Just because she didn't want to marry him didn't mean she wanted to see him hurt.

He kept up with the leg exercise. "I must call the palace."

The *palace*. Right.

Because he was a sheik. And she was a Wyoming doctor who was still paying off her student loans. A giant gap stretched between them, a gorge that could not be bridged: different countries, different cultures, different social status.

And all that distance didn't *have* to be bridged, really. Because they were not going to be part of each other's lives in any meaningful way. There was no way in hell that she was marrying him. No way was she going to be Mrs. Sheik.

He could make his calls, have his people come and pick him up, the sooner the better. Then she was out of here. She had a baby to bring into this world, and a carefully planned life to live.

She hesitated for a moment, a small part of her wishing for the impossible.

Then he said, "I'll assign you a secretary who will tie up all loose ends for you here. You won't be coming back to the U.S. for a while. I'll hire a manager to take care of this cabin and any other property you own if you wish to keep them."

On second thought, the smartest thing might be to leave before his people got here. She didn't think he would take her against her will, but then again, she wouldn't stake her life on it.

"How nice of you," she said, while at the same time she thought, *Time to ditch the sheik.*

THE MAN GIVING the orders rattled off a residential address for one of the quiet suburbs of Dumont, the perfect hiding place to move his plans to the next stage. "Use GPS. You shouldn't have any trouble finding it. Make sure you're not followed."

"Yes, sir." The man taking the orders hesitated. "At the pickup site… It looks like we're going to have some collateral damage."

"Potential for witnesses?"

"Slim to none. We're talking about a pretty remote area here."

"Good. I'll send a cleanup crew. You keep your focus on the sheik. Bring him to me. Alive if you can." He hesitated. Yes, Amir Khalid would make the perfect bait for his royal friends, but if the men were too careful around him and let him slip through their fingers once again… "Of course, if he dies, he dies. As long as he doesn't escape again, I'll be pleased."

"Yes, sir. There'll be no mistakes."

"There better not be." This was just the beginning.

"We're heading out right now, sir."

"I expect a call within the hour about whether you made a capture or made a kill."

AMIR DIALED HIS secretary at the palace, lifting his right leg and rolling his ankle at the same time. He didn't want to limp in front of his security. Or in front of Isabelle. Her resistance baffled him. In his experience, people challenged authority when they perceived it as weak. The sooner he regained his full strength, the better.

He knew what was best and he was going to take care of her and his son. As soon as she was over her feminine hysteria, she would come to see that his was the best way, the only way, really. Protocol and tradition demanded they be together. And so did he.

"I'll be outside, watering." She headed for the door.

"If you see that chopper again, come back in."

The line was picked up at the other end. "Sahed Habib, royal secretariat. How can I be of service?"

"It's Amir."

Stunned silence came first, then the sound of rapid breathing. "Are you all right, Sheik?" The always stoic voice thrilled for the first time that Amir could remember. "What happened? Everybody is looking for you."

He explained as much as he knew, then had the man fill him in on all that he'd missed. Fahad had betrayed the alliance and was dead. Amir sat stunned, the news hitting him hard. Fahad had been his best friend's cousin and head of security.

He and Efraim were going to have a long talk about this, which he didn't look forward to. But first, he had other matters to arrange.

"I need the royal physician here at the Wind

River Ranch and Resort. Put him on the next plane," he ordered, without going into detail about Isabelle.

He was careful about what he said over the phone, careful not to mention his location. If Fahad had been involved, then so could others from the palace. He sent short messages of reassurance to his sister and key people in the government about being in touch very soon, then ended that call and dialed Efraim.

"Where have you been? Do you have any idea... Never mind. Don't go anywhere. Don't talk to anyone. Don't even call the police. There's danger—" The line went dead. No battery power left on the phone. He grunted with frustration as he slapped the phone onto the counter and headed for the door. He needed the charger from Isabelle.

He caught a glimpse of her through the window. She was walking from the back of her SUV to the front and...getting in? The nervous glance she cast toward the cabin confirmed his sudden suspicions. She was sneaking out on him once again.

"Isabelle!" He lunged for the door, a feat his legs weren't quite ready for, tripped and grabbed on to the shelf by the coat hanger, pulled the stack of blankets off it by accident. The hunting rifle that had been hidden under them crashed to the floor with a clatter.

So it was nothing but sheer luck that when the beaten-up black van tore up the road, leaving a dust cloud in its wake, he had a gun in hand. An exceedingly good thing, since the second the van stopped, the men jumping from it opened fire.

They weren't playing around. Judging from their weapons, they were stone-cold professionals, here to do business.

Isabelle dove inside the SUV as best as she could, considering her round belly. He provided her with cover and prayed that she got out of there before she got hurt. Instead, she drove to pick him up, tires squealing.

"Go! I'll hold them off." He took aim and squeezed off another shot.

"I swear if you don't get in…" She looked scared to death but determined, steel glinting in her blue eyes.

And he didn't have any choice but to jump into the car. Hesitating would have put their lives in even more danger.

Then Isabelle was peeling out of there, driving like mad down some trail that went behind the cabin.

"Duck!" he yelled just in time, as a hail of bullets hit the back window and it exploded.

Chapter Three

"Are you hit?" Isabelle swerved to avoid a pothole the size of a meteor crater, her voice an octave higher than usual. She was used to hospital emergencies, but a shoot-out at her father's old cabin was a whole different category. Normally, she had to deal only with the aftermath of violence, sewing up cuts after a fight or removing bullets. Being in the middle of a battle was a whole other kettle of fish.

"No. You?" Amir pulled himself back into the car at last. He'd been hanging half out the window, firing at the men behind them like some Old West gunslinger, keeping them pinned to their positions, doing interesting things to the hospital gown he was wearing.

Good thing she wasn't watching.

He was not a sheltered palace royal, obviously. "I'm fine. Where did you learn to shoot like that?"

He gave her a hard look. "You know, all Arabs are not terrorists. My father was an excellent hunter. He used to take me with him."

She glanced into the rearview mirror. "I wasn't implying anything."

The van gave pursuit, but they didn't know every dip in the old country road as she did, and the "dirt-bike obstacle course" nature of it slowed them down. "I'm guessing those are the men who want you dead," she said as calmly as she was capable. "Who are they?"

"I don't recognize a single face." He scowled. "Are you sure you are all right? You didn't hit your belly?"

"I'm a doctor. I can monitor my own condition." She didn't need him to take care of her. She needed to be far away from him.

She glanced in the rearview mirror again. "They're getting closer." As they neared the main highway, the old road got better and better, proving less of an impediment.

He rifled through the glove compartment. "I'm out of bullets. Do you have any more?"

"Sure, and check for that grenade launcher under your seat." She rolled her eyes. Just because she lived in the country, it didn't mean she was some militia chick. Although, at the moment, maybe just one extra cartridge would have been nice.

He actually checked under the seat.

"Oh, for heaven's sake. You know, all Americans are not gun crazy."

"You had a gun."

"My father had a gun. And I don't think he ever shot anything."

She reached the main road at last and pulled onto it, seeing only one other car way far ahead, and one way far behind them. "Hang on."

She floored the gas and the SUV shot forward at an even greater speed. She didn't much care about the speed limit. The cops pulling her over would be a good thing right now. Of course, the cops were never around when you needed them.

"Do you have the phone?"

"I left it at the cabin. Dead battery." He shoved his long fingers through his jet-black hair.

She really needed a new battery for that phone. This one was getting worse and worse at holding a charge. Of course, she might not live long enough to have to worry about that again. She gripped the wheel tight and passed a beaten-up pickup that was towing a horse trailer.

"I should be driving." Frustration and disapproval sat clear on Amir's face. "We should switch."

"Because I look ready to perform acrobatics in tight places?"

"You don't like doing what I tell you," he observed with obvious displeasure.

"Tough chickpeas."

"What's that?"

"Something my father used to say. Sit back and hang on until we lose these idiots. I'm going to have to handle this, because there's no other way."

He really *had* been a lot more agreeable when he'd been in a coma. They'd had a couple of really good talks. She'd talked. He listened very sweetly, even when she'd berated him for having concealed his true identity. She'd also run some ideas by him about the future and her plans to raise her son. His silent support had been much appreciated.

At the moment, he was eyeing the steering wheel as if he were considering grabbing it.

"Don't make me go for the eject button," she warned.

He folded his arms in front of him, the tight look on his face betraying just how little he appreciated her sense of humor. Odd how for the last nine months, she'd been thinking about him as a dashing foreigner who'd been all fun and games. Better put that down to hormonal brain damage.

"If you want to do something, put some clothes on. I have a bag of my father's old things in the back." She'd planned to drop it off at the Salvation Army on her way to her doctor's appointment today.

He reached back and pulled the bag forward, selected a dark shirt and a pair of jeans, then shoved the rest back.

"The jeans will probably be too big in the waist. There are a couple of belts in the bottom of the bag." She kept her gaze straight ahead as he dressed— jeans on bare bottom. Completely straight ahead. As if her life depended on it. Which it did.

The temperature in the car rose a few degrees. She cursed her peripheral vision. She so didn't need any more tantalizing images of Amir in her brain. At the speed she was driving, it simply wasn't safe.

He turned fully toward her when he was done,

bracing himself on the dashboard with his right hand. "I'm going to ask you some questions. Do not be offended."

She let out a slow breath. "That's not a good start, is it?"

He scowled some more. Where did he get that? She didn't remember him scowling once during the two days they'd spent together in the Emerald Suite. He'd been fun-loving, curious and imaginative. *Very* imaginative.

"Did you have anything to do with that limousine exploding?"

Her hands tightened on the steering wheel. "No."

"Did you know who I was back when we first met?"

"No. And I wish I still didn't know." His royal background only complicated things.

He paused before his next question. "Do you want me dead?"

Oh, for heaven's sake. "I spent the last month of my life taking care of you." She glared at him for a second. She couldn't afford to take her eyes off the road longer than that. "Do I want you back in Jamala? Oh, yes. Dead? No. And that's an insult, by the way." She glanced into the rearview mirror. Their pursuers were even closer now than the last time she'd checked.

"I need to know without a doubt—"

"Could you not accuse me of attempted murder in the middle of a high-speed, armed chase? It's the first time I'm doing something like this."

He muttered something under his breath. Sounded like he was once again lamenting the fact that he wasn't sitting behind the wheel.

And she didn't say anything back. She was a doctor. She was used to dealing with the U.S. health-care system. She was used to disrespect. She was used to frustration. She was just going to treat him as a difficult patient or a snotty health-insurance representative. She was going to take the high road if it killed her.

She kept her focus on the road as miles whizzed by. Her game was to put as many cars between her SUV and the black van as possible. All the hand-eye coordination and quick reflexes she'd gained practicing general surgery now came in pretty handy.

"I'm going to trust you," he said out of the blue, just as she passed a tractor-trailer.

"Whoopee."

"Do you mock me?" He sounded startled.

She wanted to beat her head against the steering wheel. "I wouldn't dare." First he asked her to marry him; *then* he decided to trust her? She almost pointed out the insanity of that, before she realized that he hadn't actually *asked* her to marry him. He'd told her.

She gritted her teeth, while he seemed to have fallen into regal, disdainful silence. The black van was still following them, but at least their pursuers were no longer shooting. A definite improvement.

"Why did they find me now?" he asked after a

while. "Why not before? They had four weeks to track me down."

She hadn't had time to think about that yet. She considered his question as she took the next exit, heading for Dumont, hoping to lose her pursuers in a maze of narrow streets and alleys.

"I made some calls yesterday," she confessed. It was the only possible link she could come up with. "This baby could come any minute. You couldn't be left alone at the cabin while I went into the hospital to give birth. You needed someone to run the medical equipment."

He thought that over. "How did you get all that equipment together with short notice?"

"My father recently passed away from cancer. He wanted to die at the cabin, so I had everything set up for him." Including two generators, plus the sun panels on the roof. "He had a twenty-four-hour nurse, and I went out there every day after my shift ended." Her father had desperately tried to hang on long enough to meet his grandson.

Moisture gathered in her eyes. She blinked it away. "With the funeral and all, I hadn't had a chance to call for pickup yet when you showed up." It hadn't been an easy summer.

"I'm sorry about your father." His tone was subdued.

She nodded, driving as fast as she could while still keeping control of the vehicle.

"You made sure your father was taken care of.

Then you cared for me. You are an extraordinary woman."

Probably trying to butter her up for something. But when she glanced over, she saw only surprise on his face. Which irked her. "Did you think I would abandon my father at the end of his life? Or that I would leave the father of my child bleeding on the road?"

"I was giving you a compliment. We didn't have sufficient time to fully discover each other before. Many things about you are new to me. I'm looking forward to getting to know you better." He looked surprised at that, too, as if the words coming out of his mouth were a revelation to him.

They were finally in Dumont and she took the first bigger road to the left, heading for a more densely populated area where enough smaller streets crisscrossed each other for a car to disappear.

"You can be part of your son's life without us having anything to do with each other." She didn't like the idea of sharing her baby—it hadn't been the way she'd planned things—but, fine, he had the right, and her child would want to know his father. She could be flexible. To a point. "Once he's old enough to be in school, he could go to Jamala for a week each summer."

"My son will not grow up in a broken home," he said in a tone he must have used for royal decrees, authoritative and final.

How did they get back to the subject of marriage again? "Let's talk about something else before my blood pressure sends us hurtling into a phone pole, okay?"

"Do you have problems with your blood pressure? You said the pregnancy was going well," he accused her.

"No problems whatsoever before you woke up." She gritted her teeth. He got to her like no other, pushing all the wrong buttons.

Funny how nine months ago he'd been pushing all the right ones. And then some. She bit her lip. She so needed to stop thinking about those insane two days.

She glanced at the rearview mirror. No black van in sight. She careened into a back alley and slowed, surveyed the row of back doors, which she knew led to kitchens and laundry rooms, swerved to avoid the garbage cans lined up by the road. Not a person in sight, only a cat sauntering in front of her.

She brought the SUV to a complete stop. "Do we try to find a phone and call the police?"

He shook his head.

"Who then? FBI? CIA? Department of Defense?"

"No."

"Of course not." Because that would have been easy. "Then what?"

He looked darkly ahead.

"Did you talk to anyone on the phone before the battery went dead?"

He nodded.

"Bad news?"

He nodded again.

"Can I just remind you that you recently decided to trust me? Some information would be nice. We're in this together."

His face darkened further. "I apologize for that."

She didn't want apologies. She wanted a plan. "Why can't we call the police?"

"Efraim said… The phone gave out before he could explain. No police."

"Fine. Then we find a phone and you can call this Efraim again."

"Yes. That would be best. My friends will send a team for us. We'll be safe at the resort. Once the royal physician arrives, he'll take you to Jamala under guard. I might have to stay here for a day or two. There are international relations to consider. I might have duties left still with things we came here to accomplish."

She wasn't thrilled at the idea of his security staff arriving and taking control of her. "Or, how about this? Why wait for anyone? With armed madmen looking for us out there, I'm thinking time is of the essence. I can take you to Wind River and your friends. Then we part ways. I'll drop you off at the gate."

"We must not fight about this. Stress is not good for you or my son. You should be reasonable." He had the gall to reproach her.

Enough steam gathered in her head to fill the steam bath at the resort's fancy spa. She gave Amir her sweetest smile. "If you don't like my plan, you can always get out of the car right here."

He didn't have the chance to respond. The black van appeared at the other end of the alley, flying toward them, motor roaring.

No room to turn the SUV around.

No time to inch out of the narrow alley backward, slowly.

They were trapped.

BEFORE ANY BULLETS could fly, Amir bolted from the car, Isabella right next to him. He hated, absolutely hated, that he'd brought danger to her. He couldn't believe she had the wherewithal to grab her purse first, but she had it with her as they busted in through the back door of the nearest house. They ran through a small, empty kitchen, then a living room, a half-dozen cats scattering from their path and giving them dirty looks.

"Is that you, Brian?" a woman called from upstairs, hardwood floor creaking as she moved around. "Where have you been?"

They burst through the front door without answering, then scrambled across the road, into a crowded bar that smelled like smoke and beer, the Jukebox blaring a country song he wasn't familiar with. They slowed to make their way to the back without drawing too much attention. In seconds they were in another alley. His muscles were shaking; his breathing was heavy. He cursed his weak legs, which slowed them both.

"You made it this far. You can do it." Isabelle took him by the hand to pull him after her.

Male pride said he should pull away and make his way unaided. But her small hands felt incredible around his fingers, the feel of her warm skin giving him a jolt, bringing back memories. He left his hand in hers and ignored his screaming muscles.

The faces of their pursuers danced in his mind. This time, he'd made a point of taking a good look. He didn't recognize any of them. They didn't look Jamalan. They looked American.

Yet his secretary had said that Fahad had worked for the enemy. Did some xenophobic American group pay Fahad to sabotage the summit?

Isabelle pulled him forward relentlessly. He kept looking back, but the men must have gotten hung up somewhere, because they weren't following. Maybe they were still searching the bar.

"Where are we going?" Again, it galled him that she would have to save him and take the lead. But it was obvious that she was familiar with this place as she made her way to a specific back door.

She had her key ring in her hand, picked a key and shoved it into the old lock, opened the door, pulled him in, then locked the door behind them. They were in a narrow white hallway, breathing hard.

He was tense and not sure if they could relax yet, if the building was safe. "What is this place?"

"My father practiced family medicine here before he retired. Hasn't been rented out since. I keep forgetting to give back my duplicate key."

She led the way and they reached a waiting room

that was lit by the last of the setting sun. There were upholstered chairs stacked on top of each other, dust everywhere. The door to one of the exam rooms was open. He spotted a phone on the wall and went for it. He needed to reach Efraim, needed immediate backup.

No dial tone.

Just when he would have banged the receiver against the wall, Isabelle took it gently away from him. "I'm sure they canceled phone service when they closed the office. Would you sit down, please?"

That he needed to sit and rest annoyed him. In fact, annoyance and frustration seemed to be the main theme of the hours since he'd awakened. "How long before I'm back like I was before?"

"At least a couple of weeks. You're doing amazingly well, all things considered. One might almost think you're too stubborn to be sick."

He couldn't help a small grin. "Stubborn?" Yes, he'd probably been that way with her and worse. Not that she wasn't impossibly stubborn herself, but he was going to be a gentleman and not mention that again. "You are not seeing me at my best," he allowed.

She outright laughed at him. "Really?"

The sweet sound of her laughter had a way of sneaking straight into the middle of his chest. Her face lit up. Her silky hair had fallen across her forehead in their mad dash, but now she brushed the dark strands out of her face. Her blue eyes shone in the dim light of dusk.

"You're beautiful." The words just slipped out.

She raised an eyebrow. "I'm still not entering into some arranged marriage."

"Nobody arranged anything for us. This is not something set up by our parents. We should both choose this marriage because it's the right thing to do. It is the only honorable course of action. My country and my people expect no less from me."

"Marrying for protocol's sake? Living some happy royal farce for the media?"

He rose and strode to her, turned her to face him. Her amazing eyes were wary; her bottom lip was bruised from biting. Her face had been on his mind every day since she'd left him. Her body—sans clothes—had been a major player in his dreams.

"If I married for protocol, according to the wishes of the Council, I would marry for alliance. I would marry a princess for her father's wealth and influence," he informed her.

Nothing wrong with that. Last he heard, his friend Prince Stefan had been considering just such a marriage to Princess Daria. Alliances were important. Yet, he couldn't say he was upset by the turn of events that would make Isabelle his bride. He could see them being happy. He could see them doing a great many things. A number of them involved being naked.

"Sounds good to me. You should try and keep this Council happy. They sound important."

"They'll be happy that I finally secured an heir." They'd been bugging him about that from the moment he'd taken the throne. "This might not be the marriage they had in mind, but they won't protest it."

"*I* protest it. I'm not entering into a fake marriage so you can parade my son around as your heir."

"Nothing about our marriage would be fake, I promise you that, Isabelle," he told her before he kissed her.

Chapter Four

His lips were firm on hers and warm, coaxing. If the kiss had been the claiming sort, him trying to prove that she *would* belong to him, she could have resisted. But Amir's tender seduction had Isabelle's head spinning.

His hands came to her nonexistent waist. Probably felt like he was hugging a whale. She shied away, but he pulled her right back, one hand moving to rest on her belly. The baby kicked against his palm. For a second he stilled; then he deepened the kiss with a surge of new emotion.

Her knees were as shaky as his had to be. She shouldn't be doing this. Her giving in was bound to give him ideas that she was agreeing to his insane plans about them getting married. It gave the wrong impression altogether, not to mention that it was medically irresponsible. She was his doctor for the time being. He needed rest. Lots of it.

She pulled back once again, although with a reluctance that she couldn't hide from him. "You should lie down."

The roguish grin that split his face took her breath away. She knew that look. She'd seen that look on the prince of Persia's face nearly nonstop for two days.

He moved toward the rolled-up carpet in the corner, capturing her hand and drawing her with him.

"Alone." She dug her heels in and extricated herself, despite the thrill that ran through her. "If you overtax yourself, it will slow your recovery."

"Let me worry about my recovery." But he let her go with a displeased frown, stepped over to the carpet and folded it in two, sat down. "I don't like this. I just woke up after a month of rest. How can I be this tired?"

"A little thing called muscle atrophy. It's a miracle that you're even out of bed. Believe me, this is not your usual coma recovery. Some people need weeks just to get on their feet. You should sleep."

"And you?" He held out his hand again.

She couldn't say she wasn't tempted. Her back ached. Lying down for a while, curled up against Amir, sounded like heaven. Which was reason enough not to do it. So instead of stepping forward, she stepped away.

"You're mad at me," he said.

"No." The response came on reflex. She was a doctor and she'd been taking care of him. Technically, he was her patient. A doctor didn't get mad at her patient. Period. It would have been unprofessional. But the unqualified *no* was a lie. She drew a deep breath. "I don't want to be."

"Are you mad because I left the country without finding you, or because I came back? Or because I'm putting your life in danger?"

"Do you have an easier question?"

"Are you not the least bit happy that we're together again?"

"We're not *together* together."

"Are you not happy that I survived the explosion and came out of the coma?"

"Very happy."

A pleased smile stretched on his face. He held his hands out for her once again.

She took another step back. She wasn't going to fall into some idiotic fantasy that he needed her, that he wanted her for anything but his precious heir. Whatever attraction there was between them, she was perfectly capable of ignoring.

"I'll look around and see what I can find to make us more comfortable. We should stay put until morning. Whoever is after you, they know we no longer have a car to get away in. They're probably watching the streets."

He lay down and folded his hands under his head, stared up at the ceiling, his jaw tight with tension. "I should be fighting my enemies, not taking a nap."

He wasn't the easiest patient she'd ever seen. "I hope for the royal physician's sake that you're not often sick."

"Never," he said, as if that was a matter of pride.

Then he turned to her. "How seriously was I injured in the explosion?"

She headed into her father's office. "Bad enough to keep me worried, but not life threatening. Started with a pretty high GSC score and kept getting better. I didn't think you'd take this long to wake. Respiratory functions were normal from the beginning, steady heartbeat, good BP. Some eye movement, muscle response to pain."

She opened the desk drawers one by one and found them empty. "A light coma, all things considered. I couldn't have kept you out of the hospital if you were any worse. I really shouldn't have, anyway. Could have ended up being a huge mistake."

Basically, she'd gambled with his life. She hated that, even if it was per his request. Providing less than the absolute best possible care went against her training as well as her personal moral code. But she had believed that he might be in even bigger danger if he wasn't in hiding. That explosion had been pretty convincing. And now those men chasing them and shooting at them drove the point home, telling her that she'd done the right thing.

"You saved my life," he said in a tone of absolute certainty that chased away the last of her lingering doubts.

"You really don't know who wants you dead?" She opened the closet and found a white doctor's jacket, ran her fingers along her father's name on the pocket, blinking back sudden tears. She wished she could ask her father's advice on the mess she'd gotten herself into. She wished she could ask him what he thought of Amir.

The two were nothing alike on the outside, yet similar in some ways on the inside. Her father had been an honorable man, a gentle man. Didn't smoke, didn't drink, didn't cuss. The worst he ever said, if someone really got his dander up, was, "Tough chickpeas" or "Blazing buzzards."

"I suppose, a lot of people want to see me out of the picture," Amir was saying out in the waiting room. "Some extremists in my country would rather see me dead than sign a deal with the United States. Some people right here are convinced that I have some terrorist agenda just because the majority of Jamalans are Muslim."

"So why did you come? Is whatever you're trying to do here important enough to risk your life?" She couldn't imagine that he didn't have everything right at home that he needed for a life of amazing power and luxury. He had palaces to enjoy and a whole army protecting him. He was royalty. He probably had beautiful women lined up ten deep, hoping to marry him.

"I'm not going to 'run and hide' because there are people out there motivated by hate and fear who are all too willing to spread and believe lies about me."

"I didn't say 'run and hide.' Just keep a low profile." She hated the idea of him getting hurt. Which didn't mean that she was developing any kind of feelings for him. She hated the idea of anyone getting hurt. Plus, he was the father of her baby. "You don't need to make yourself into a giant target."

"Good people must never give up and lock themselves away from the world's problems. Moderates from each side must cooperate. The truth must be put out there and repeated as many times as necessary. The radical voice cannot be the only one to be heard."

Another closet held two nurses' uniforms. One of them had a forgotten stethoscope in its pocket. She found a box of unopened tongue depressors on a shelf. She closed the door, frustrated, and moved on to the examining rooms. "We have a saying like that. 'All that is necessary for evil to triumph is for good men to do nothing.'"

"Which is exactly why my friends and I all came despite the dangers. The exact reason why we refuse to be defeated. Once a person starts running from evil, there's no stopping."

She glanced at him through the open door. Even barely recovered from a coma and flat on his back, he was still the embodiment of heroic. She felt something deep inside her respond to him. *Stupid, stupid, stupid.* They barely knew each other. And if he got wind of any softening on her part, he would double his efforts to convince her to agree to the loveless marriage scheme his misplaced honor demanded.

Because, okay, he'd made his point about passion with that kiss. Their marriage wouldn't be without passion. And, to be truthful, her body thrilled at just the thought of it. But what about love? That he hadn't said a single word about love didn't escape her notice.

She focused back on her search, turning her back to him, refusing to let him distract her. Empty drawers. Empty shelves. Stacks of marketing materials from pharmaceutical companies. By the time she was done looking around, finding nothing whatsoever that could help them in any way, Amir was asleep, his breathing even.

Darkness had fallen outside.

She stepped to the window, keeping in the cover of the dusty curtains. An old Ford pickup thundered up the street. Traffic had lessened, but by no means stopped. No black van. People were still out and about, and she had no idea whether their pursuers were among them. They could have ditched the van, could be looking for her and Amir on foot now. There were four of them. For all she knew, they were as familiar with Dumont as she was. She might have found shelter for the night, but she and Amir were far from safe.

She went to the back and cracked the door, looked out into the alley. The narrow, dark space was deserted and filled with the stench of garbage cans that had been heating in the sun all day. A neon light, advertising a popular brand of beer, flickered above the solid steel door of the bar across from her, the door propped open with a brick to let some of the smoke out. Country music wafted in the night air.

She stepped back inside, passed Amir quietly and went straight to the office to put on one of the nurses' uniforms, Ashunda's. Her father's favorite, she'd been a no-nonsense gal from Detroit, as tall as an Amazon and voluptuous, which allowed Isabelle to fasten all but the middle button.

There was a small medical center a block away. Nobody at the bar would think that her uniform was strange. Clint's was the only place that had takeout food in the neighborhood. Even her father used to grab lunch there.

She hung the stethoscope around her neck, then twisted her hair up into a bun to further change her appearance, grabbed her wallet, tiptoed by Amir. He didn't even stir. She checked the back alley again. When she was satisfied that she wouldn't be seen by anyone, she darted over to the bar's back door and slipped in, hoping and praying that Amir's enemies weren't in there, waiting.

"YOU LOST HIM." The man stood in the shadows of the basement, the four idiots he'd hired for the job lined up under the single lightbulb that hung from the ceiling. Maybe he'd made a mistake in switching teams. But the Russians had gained too much visibility. The royals knew Aleksei Verovick was involved. And if they had a name, there was a risk that the job could be traced back to the source.

"They won't get far." The loser who was the local degenerates' team leader dared to talk back to him.

"I'm afraid we have a matter of loss of confidence

here." He pulled his gun, silencer already in place, and put a bullet through the man's head, his attention already on the others as the body folded to the floor. He aimed the gun at the next one. "Can you guarantee that the matter will be handled today?"

The shorter man paled in the dim light. "Yes, sir."

"Good." He put the gun away. "Congratulations. You are the new boss."

The dimwit's shoulders slumped with relief.

"Which means, the next time something goes wrong, you'll be the one I'll hold responsible."

The fear flashed back into the man's eyes. Good. A little fear was a healthy thing for business. A lot of fear was even better.

The man nearly stuttered as he rushed to say, "That won't happen, sir. We're watching their car and have it tagged, too. The second the sheik moves, we'll have him."

AMIR WOKE TO the smell of food coming from a container next to him. The place was dark, very little moonlight coming in the windows, so a moment passed before he could orient himself.

Isabelle was coming from one of the other rooms. She had her hair up, the slim curve of her neck revealed. "How do you feel?"

"Where did you get this from?" He sat up. "You shouldn't have left."

Anger took him swiftly at the thought that while he'd slept, she'd been out there unprotected. They couldn't trust the police; they couldn't even trust his own security. For the time being, they were all alone in this. She didn't seem to grasp the gravity of their situation. The men who'd been shooting at them weren't playing around. They shot to kill.

"I know this neighborhood," she was saying with exaggerated patience, which set his teeth even more on edge. "I was careful. I only stepped over to the bar for some mild chicken wings. You need protein."

"And you and my son need to be protected. You must accept my protection, Isabelle." What little he could provide at the moment. Things would change once he put together a trustworthy security detail.

She stopped moving and pulled her shoulders straight. "We should probably talk about this. Look, the way I was during those two days in your suite…" She colored a little. "That was under extraordinary circumstances. I'm never that spontaneous. I'm never that irresponsible, never that easy to talk into doing wild things. *This* is how I really am."

Her hands moved in an impatient gesture. "You must accept that I'm not some obedient little thing who will bow to your every whim. A person doesn't get to be a surgeon if she's a type-B personality. I'm stubborn, independent as hell, and value my freedom more than I value my life. Whatever happened between us all those months ago was the exception to the rule, an aberration. Consider it temporary insanity."

He could do little more than stare at her. Her insubordination was extraordinary. Yet he wasn't angry. He was turned on, immediately and completely.

In fact, his body was making all sorts of needs known to him all at once. His stomach growled as she pushed the bucket of wings toward him, along with a wad of paper napkins. He remembered those slim fingers caressing his heated skin and wanted that again with a fierce longing.

She could be as stubbornly independent as she wanted; he could handle that. But when he returned to Jamala, she would be going with him.

"I got a few bottles of water. Some to drink, some to flush the toilet." She sat on the corner of the carpet, all business, oblivious to the storm that swirled inside him. "Now that you're off the IV fluids, it's important that you keep yourself hydrated."

She was right about that. Water and food had to be his priorities. He needed to regain his strength before he could do anything else. He didn't realize how hungry he'd been until he bit into the first wing. Flavor exploded in his mouth. "You will not go anywhere else without me," he said between two bites.

Her eyebrows drew together. Her face held a world of warning.

He ignored that. "Yes, because you're a woman and also because you're nine-months pregnant, and because there are armed men out there." He couldn't stand the thought of her getting hurt because of him. "I'm going to protect you," he promised.

"You're my patient. I'm supposed to protect you."

That didn't even make any sense. He was the sheik, the father of his nation, the supreme protector. He shook his head, not wanting to waste more energy on a pointless argument. He ate a dozen more wings before he took a break to drink.

She waited until he was finished before helping herself. "I probably shouldn't. I'll be in heartburn city by morning, but they don't have too many health-food choices at the bar."

They finished the bucket in silence; then she cleaned up, quick and efficient despite her large belly.

He wanted his hands on her, wanted to feel his son moving around. "Come lie next to me." He made room for her. "It's as uncomfortable as it looks, but better than the bare floor."

"No thanks. I'll sit in a chair."

And sneak off again the second he closed his eyes? "I want you next to me. I insist. Or I'll stay up all night to make sure you do not go anywhere."

Even in the dim moonlight he could see as she rolled her eyes. "Fine." She lay down next to him, as far away as the folded carpet allowed. "But only because I know you're stubborn enough to do that, and as your doctor I have to make sure you get adequate rest. This is a medical concession. Don't read too much into it."

He smiled into the darkness, then reached out

and pulled her closer, her back to his front, leaving his hand resting on her belly. He wished his son would kick again. "You can't blame me for not trusting you. You've left me at the resort before. And you would have left me at the cabin."

"You made contact with your people. You no longer needed me. You do realize I have my own life to live?"

Again, she spoke nonsense. She carried his son. Separate lives no longer existed for either of them. He ran his hand over her round belly, fascinated by the shape. His son was in there. Warmth spread in his chest at the thought. Her proximity sent warmth spreading through the rest of his body.

Tomorrow he would find a phone and call the resort again, establish contact with Efraim and the others. Tonight belonged to Isabelle. He was grateful for having found her, for his son and for the grace that all three of them were still alive and unharmed.

Life was full of irony. They didn't call him the Black Sheep Sheik for nothing. He'd had his hellraising days during his misspent youth. He had taken the reins of his country reluctantly but gave it his all once he'd taken them. The two-day fling with a beautiful stranger in Wyoming had been his way of going back to his carefree life for another taste. No complications, no commitments. They didn't even know each other's names.

To be completely truthful, when he'd returned to Wyoming with the others a month ago, he'd been looking for more of the same. In hindsight, he'd probably been a fool to think that another fling would have been enough. Isabelle wasn't the type of woman a sane man would let go if he had a choice, baby or no baby.

And now here they were.

"When I call my secretary again tomorrow, I'm going to ask the man to assemble a committee to plan the royal wedding." On the few occasions when he'd thought of that in the past, he usually shuddered. Now he was looking forward to it.

"Keep dreaming," she said in a dry tone, failing to show even a smidgen of respect for his wishes.

He would convince her to see things his way. He wanted this wedding and he would have it. A sharp departure from his wilder younger days.

It wasn't that he'd grown up that much. The prospect of fast cars or a good sword fight with one of his friends still got his blood humming. Nor was it that he had a potential heir, although he considered that an undeserved blessing.

Isabelle made all the difference. She was the only woman he'd ever met that he could picture by his side for the next many decades. And, of course, she was the only woman he'd ever met who wanted nothing to do with him. The irony of fate.

He leaned forward and pressed his lips to her neck, to the soft spot where it met her shoulder. He remembered that spot. He planned on having regular contact with it. "Do you remember the night we met?"

"I should have dressed as a nun. No, never mind. I can't regret those two days." She rolled to her back so she could look at him. "How did everything become such a huge mess? Why couldn't you have turned out to be a normal, everyday person? A hospital administrator would have been great. I would have even settled for a pharmaceutical rep. I wouldn't have liked all the traveling, but I would have supported it."

So she liked the man behind the trappings of royalty. Optimism spread through him. "I'm a normal, everyday person. Behind the title, I'm just a man."

"If only it were that easy."

"Then don't overcomplicate it."

She closed her eyes. He kissed one lid and moved to the other. He wanted her, now, in every way a man could want a woman. Except, he wasn't sure how that would work with the baby. He reached for the last of his restraint. For now, the feel of her in his arms would have to be enough.

But she seemed intent on denying him even this. She placed a hand against his chest and pushed him away. "Don't do this."

"I can't seem to help myself." That she wasn't as happy about them finding each other again as he was stung. Isabelle no longer wanted him. Frustration welled in his chest.

He kept an arm around her. "Sleep. All this running around cannot be helpful in your condition."

"I'm the doctor here. I give the rest orders," she

mumbled. But soon her breathing evened and she was asleep.

He watched her for a while in the moonlight. She was even more beautiful than he remembered. She had delicate cheekbones and shapely brows, blazing eyes when they were open. Her mouth was a thing of beauty, her full bottom lip much abused. When she was nervous, she had a tendency to chew it, the only sign of weakness she ever allowed.

She was intelligent, practical, with a brave spirit. She'd handled that chase as well as one of his security guards. She'd found them shelter and food. No, she was not obedient. But if she were anything less than what she was, they would probably be dead by now.

He thought that revelation over. She was what she was, and truth be told, he liked what she was. More than liked. She wouldn't be an accessory on the throne, by his side. She would be a partner. Yes, he had taken on the yoke of ruling willingly and had expected to shoulder it alone. But the thought of her being by his side all through it suddenly made him feel lighter than he had since his parents' death. She would make an amazing princess, if only he could make her see that.

He would. First thing tomorrow morning. They would be safe at the resort and his friends would be there to help him. No mortal woman could resist that much charm. The five of them together were a force to be reckoned with. She would see reason.

He rose quietly and moved to the window without making a sound, scanned the street. He couldn't see the black van. He picked up a stack of chairs and blocked the back door, just in case. Then he went back to Isabelle and wrapped his arm around her again, breathing in her sweet scent.

He fell asleep with visions of her on the throne, next to him, in his arms in the royal ballroom, twirling to the music, in his bed—naked. She laughed that laugh of hers that warmed his heart like nothing on earth could. She came into his arms willingly. He sank deeper into the dream.

He woke to the sun shining into his eyes. Isabelle's place next to him was empty. Only a stack of coins and a note waited for him.

The bar across the back alley will open in a couple of hours. They have a pay phone. Call your people. Be safe.

He bolted straight up, swearing like a desert bandit.

His future princess had left him.

Chapter Five

Her car had been stolen.

Isabelle groaned with frustration as she looked up and down the alley where they'd left the vehicle the night before. Nothing. *Okay, don't think stolen.* Her mind had a habit of going to the worst-case scenario, an occupational hazard. In the O.R., she had to think in terms of the worst-case scenario at each and every surgery and imagine exactly what she would do if that happened. In the O.R., she had to be ready for whatever came her way. Right now, however, she needed some positive thinking.

Think towed. Towed would be manageable.

The bar wasn't open yet, so she couldn't go use their pay phone. Nor would she have wanted to run into Amir in there. She had to find another phone. Without being seen by whomever was after Amir.

She walked back out of the alley and headed for one of the busier streets. She was still wearing the nurses' uniform. She sidled into the first clothing store she found, Lainey's Western Outfitters, and bought a large shirt, plus a cowboy hat that hid her pinned-up hair and most of her face. She picked up a pair of large hoop earrings, which provided a little more cover and distraction.

She didn't exactly look stylish, but at least she didn't look like she had when that black van had pulled into her front yard. She even exchanged her red purse for a brown one with horseshoe prints on the side and tassels on the bottom. If those men caught sight of her on the street, they might not recognize her like this. Honestly, she barely recognized herself.

"You wouldn't have a public phone in here, would you?" she asked the gum-chewing salesgirl after she paid.

"Sorry."

Figured. "A phone book?"

"Got that." The girl, seventeen or eighteen, slapped the big yellow book on the table, then pushed back her pink-glittered cowboy hat a little.

"I think my car was towed," Isabelle explained, trying to remain positive, as she flipped through the pages. Dumont was a pretty decent town with not much of a crime rate.

A few seconds passed before she found the right page. Only one towing outfit in town. That made things simple. She copied the phone number onto the back of her store receipt.

The salesgirl pulled a cordless phone from behind the counter and set it in front of Isabelle. "Might as well call. The boss probably won't mind a local number."

"Are you sure?"

"You can't be walking around all day. Us knocked-up girls have to stick together."

And sure enough, now that Isabelle looked, she did see a little baby bump hanging out of the skimpy top that left too much of the salesgirl's breasts and midriff bare.

She made the call and confirmed that they had her car. *Yea for positive thinking.* She could pick it up anytime for a fifty-dollar fee. She was so relieved, she didn't even mind the money.

"Wanna call your man to come and pick you up?" the girl offered when Isabelle handed the phone back.

"Thanks. No man."

"Mine's out on the rodeo circuit. He'll be back in two weeks." The girl smiled and her crooked front teeth made her look even younger.

"What's your due date?"

"End of winter, I think."

"Hasn't your doctor told you exactly?"

"I only work here a few hours a week. I don't make that much money."

"The hospital has a free prenatal clinic. If you go in, they'll give you a checkup at no cost. They also have free vitamins."

"Yeah? Maybe. Whatever." The gum in her mouth kept snapping.

Isabelle held back the urge to push and prayed that the girl would do the right thing. She thanked her for all the help, then shrugged into the oversize shirt and put on her hat before she left the shop, looking carefully up and down the street. Didn't see anyone suspicious. Which didn't mean that they weren't out there. She kept her head down and her neck tucked in, wondering how come, if rodeo daddy had money to travel the circuit, he didn't have money for prenatal vitamins.

She stopped. Turned around. Walked back to the store and popped her head in the door. "Forgot to tell you. If you keep going to the free clinic, toward the end they give you a bunch of formula for the baby."

"Sweet."

Okay. That was all she could do. She waved at the girl and went on her way.

Amir wanting to take care of her and the baby didn't sound so terrible and controlling all of a sudden. Would she have liked him better if he had refused to even consider paternity and taken off running? Probably not. Okay, definitely not. She did like that he was honorable through and through. If only he weren't so absolutely pigheaded.

He was probably awake by now. Or maybe not. Coma patients tended to need a lot of sleep for a couple of days after they awakened. Of course, he was tougher than most anyone she knew. He'd be red-hot mad at her for leaving. But he would call the rest of the royals at the resort, they'd come with heavy security to pick him up and he would be safe.

She couldn't let him be part of her life. He was too much. He would take control. And no matter how hard she fought against that, she would eventually let him, because some part of her was tired of fighting life's battles alone and would be grateful to hand over the reins and feel taken care of and protected even if for a short break.

It was her dirty little secret. She, Isabelle Andrews, self-sufficient and independent surgeon, wanted a man in her life and his shoulder to lean on when she needed it.

Except that never worked. Believing in something like that would bring nothing but disappointment and grief. She'd seen her mother walk that treacherous path.

She walked up the street and into the first diner she came across, ordered a toasted sesame-seed bagel with ham and eggs. Plus a tall glass of orange juice. Then she waited, watching for the black van through the window, but thank God, she didn't see it. She didn't have to wait long before someone she knew walked in.

Sue Kim, the dry cleaner's wife, ordered coffee, then went to sit in the back.

Isabelle waddled over. Seemed like her belly had somehow grown an extra size overnight. Or maybe the baby was lying in a different way. The bottom of her belly felt tight today.

"Isabelle?" Sue peered under the cowboy hat. "Are you going to a party?" She eyed the semi-cowboy, semi-nurse outfit doubtfully.

"Long story. How are you, Sue?"

"Lilly got into Harvard. Did I tell you that?" She

said "Harvard" without saying any of the *r*'s, and with a slight Korean accent. "She'll be big doctor." Her face beamed with pride.

"Congratulations. That's wonderful," Isabelle said sincerely.

"How are you? When the baby coming?"

"Very soon. I'm supposed to go and see the doctor this afternoon. They check me every other day now. Of course, I just got my car towed. I was hoping I could ask you—"

"Towed?" Sue seemed outraged on her behalf. "I take you pick it up."

The waitress was coming with the coffee, but Sue waved her back, already standing. "I'll come back. I go now. Pregnant lady needs help."

Isabelle tried to protest that there was no great urgency, but Sue wouldn't hear of it. They were in the white dry-cleaner minivan before Isabelle could blink, flying down the road at a speed that defied a race-car driver, Sue cursing the busybodies at the towing company all the way.

"I miss your father," she said, then suddenly, out of the blue, added, "He a good man. You need a good man like that for your baby. You want me introduce you?"

Isabelle hid the twinge of panic with a smile. "No thanks. I'm good."

"Waiting for the father of the baby to come back. He will. You good woman."

They were at their destination before Isabelle would have had to come up with a response to that, thank God. Sue offered to wait until everything was settled, but Isabelle declined with thanks, sending her back to her coffee and her business. She didn't want to impose on the woman's time more than she had to.

She would get her car, go home, change, call the royals at the resort and tell them where she'd left Amir, in case for some reason Amir couldn't call for himself. He had said that his friends could be trusted. She wanted to make sure he was all right. Then she would work some more on the baby's room. The thought of that put a true smile on her face.

But as she turned to scan the lot, she froze on the spot. A black van was parked by the corner, hidden behind a sign for the towing company. A very familiar black van. She tried to look as non-pregnant and unlike herself as possible as she hurried across the enormous lot—keeping waddling to a minimum, ignoring the hundreds of cars, making a beeline for the office inside a rusty metal shipping container.

"Hi. I called a few minutes ago about an SUV that was picked up yesterday?"

The air inside smelled musty even with the door and window open. But at least she was out of sight and could breathe easier for the time being. The transaction was pretty straightforward, lasting less than five minutes. She showed ID and paid the fee, signed the papers.

The old man behind the beaten-up desk stopped chewing tobacco long enough to tell her where her car was. "Nothin' personal, little lady. People call that the road is blocked, we come out." He gave a toothless grin as he rocked back in a chair whose plastic seat cover was peeling.

When she exited the makeshift office, the sinister-looking black van was still waiting by the corner. She tugged her hat over her eyes and walked as fast as she could, heaved her swollen body into the car and locked the doors, shoved the key into the ignition.

Then screamed as a large shape shifted in the back, her rearview mirror showing the silhouette of a man.

"It's me. Sorry," Amir said. "I didn't want anyone to see me while I was waiting. I'm driving this time. Slide over."

Of course, she had to get out and go around. Her belly didn't exactly slide around in tight places.

"How did you get here?" She might have glared a little. She was annoyed that he'd found her so easily, and her heart was still going a mile a minute from the scare he'd given her.

"Went back to the alley where we left your car." He climbed forward and situated himself behind the steering wheel. For the well-built man that he was, he was certainly flexible. "Talked to the woman whose house we ran through. She was bringing out the garbage. I told her I was a friend of Brian's, and she was more than helpful. She told me about the tow truck."

"The black van is out front."

His lips flattened. "Wasn't there when I came. Did they follow you?"

"I don't think so. I don't know. They could have. It's not like I've been trained in how to spot a tail."

He thought for a minute. "We will leave through the back." He drove away from the office and toward the back of the lot, where a flimsy gate interrupted the chain-link fence. "I will buy you a new car," he told her, then gunned the engine.

A second later the gate was history and they were speeding down a secondary road toward the highway.

She screamed only a little. "This is my car! Are you crazy?" She did smack him on the shoulder before she could catch herself. Yes, she knew he was royalty, but at the moment, she so didn't care. The man was beyond reckless. He was certifiably crazy.

He kept his eyes on the road, with an occasional glance at the rearview mirror. He was focused completely on what he was doing, and doing it well. He could have been a super spy straight out of a movie. On one level she found that reassuring; on another it was extremely infuriating.

"Would you rather they shot us?" he asked after a few seconds.

She had enough sense not to argue his point. She hated how annoyingly levelheaded he stayed, no matter what. *She* used to be levelheaded. Composed and together at all times, ready for any emergency at the hospital. Until those pregnancy hormones took over. She no longer recognized herself these days.

She no longer recognized her life, that was for sure. Was she really the person who had hidden a foreign sheik in her father's cabin for the last month and was now becoming a fugitive with him, running from God-knew-what kind of criminals, instead of heading to the nearest police station? She needed to have her head examined. Among other things. "I still have that doctor's appointment today, and I'm not skipping it."

Which reminded her that she hadn't taken her vitamins yet today. As she reached for the bottle she kept in the glove compartment, pain sliced through her belly. She winced.

As usual, Amir didn't miss a thing. "Are you hurt?"

"Not exactly," she told him but then sucked in a deep breath as another cramp came, this one much stronger than the first.

"We're clear." Amir was looking into the rearview mirror as he sped down the road.

But at the very first crossroad, the black van was there, waiting. Amir sailed through the red light. Isabelle grabbed the door for support.

They turned down the first street, zigzagged among buildings.

"What is it?" Amir looked at her hand on her belly.

The pain had stopped, but… "It feels funny."

"Are you having the baby?"

face. "And the second one might have been just a misunderstanding."

"How can an assassination attempt be a misunderstanding?"

"Long story. There are plenty of misunderstandings in politics. Along with misinformation that's spread maliciously. People have agendas. They spread lies. Others are looking for a cause to take those lies up as banners, whether or not they understand what's going on. I was shot at once when I took the throne, based on the rumor that I would raise taxes. I had no intention of doing that. Still don't."

"How can you take this so stoically?"

He executed another hair-raising turn, then looked at her. "I'm the sheik. Not every decision I make for my country will be popular. When you rule, you must sometimes decide between a course of action that will make you popular and a course of action that will be best for your people in the long term, even if in the short term they won't like you for it."

Another small glimpse into his life, she thought. So yes, he was overbearing and bossy beyond belief, but there were also things that she admired about him. He did have strength of character, and honor. And courage.

Snap out of it.

"I hate politics." She forced herself to look at the road ahead instead of at him. She was so not falling under the spell of the dashing sheik of Jamala. Absolutely not.

He whipped her car into a gap between two buildings, jumped out and pushed one of those big community trash containers in front to block the sight of them from the busy street.

A shed blocked the other end of the alley. If they were found, the car would be trapped here. They would have to escape on foot, and she wouldn't make it far that way. She got out, wanting to at least give herself a running advantage.

He came around to her side. "How do you feel?"

"Fine." The cramps had gone away, almost as if her body had been scared straight by the chase.

She watched through the gap between the container and the wall, holding her breath, as the black van sped by. When she did breathe, the stench of rotten food threatened to turn her stomach inside out. She backed away.

"You would like Jamala," Amir said out of the blue. "It's all clear skies and endless sea. We were always at the crossroads of history. We have Egyptian ruins and remains of Roman forts. Turkish invasion left its mark, too. We belonged to the Ottoman Empire during Suleiman the Great. We have olive groves on the west side of the island and orange groves on the east." His tone was wistful.

Standing in the dank alley with the stench of garbage all around, she could see why. An orange grove on some jewel of a Mediterranean island sounded pretty good at the moment, even she had to admit. She tried to picture him there, in some palace, as sheik, in flowing white robes instead of her father's jeans and shirt. The image came to her pretty easily and stole her breath away.

Her daydreaming was interrupted by squealing tires. The stupid black van was back again.

Amir took her hand, and they ran for the other end of the alley as fast as they could, which was not very fast at all. They made a pitiful couple at the moment, neither of them exactly ready for the Olympics.

"I can't go too far," she warned him.

"You won't have to." He opened the door of the first building to their left, some sort of government office. He grinned at her. "Perfect."

They went through the metal detector without trouble.

"Where to?" the security guard asked, eyeing Amir, whose Middle Eastern heritage was unmistakable.

She glanced at the board behind the guard. "Judge Schwartz's office."

The guard nodded and sent them on their way.

They walked leisurely down the hall, turned the corner, then picked up speed.

"Do you know where you're going?"

"Away from the enemy."

She glanced back but couldn't see them. Since they were armed, no way could they get through the metal detector. She couldn't see them giving up their guns, which meant they would have to find another way into the building, or wait until Amir and she exited. Except, a building this size had many exits.

Amir strode straight ahead, keeping to his true aim, and they were out on the other side of the building, bursting through a delivery entrance that opened only from the inside. The alley where they'd left her car was to their right. The black van blocked their way, but it was empty.

Amir pushed the garbage container out of the way. "Don't get in yet."

She waited as he jumped into her car, revved the engine and plowed into the van, shoving it out of the way. Then, when he was out in the street, he opened the door for her.

She felt like crying as she climbed into the passenger seat. "I really liked this car." With the baby coming, she wasn't going to have money for another.

"I'll buy you another car," he told her again as he pulled into traffic. "I meant it when I said I was going to take care of you."

"And I meant it when I said I didn't want any of it." Fate sure had a sense of humor. Here she was, with her weird phobia of powerful men, and she had to get tangled with an extra-super-alpha male who wanted nothing but to protect her and take care of her. No way was she going to let him.

"We can go to the resort. The cramps have passed." The sooner they parted ways, the better.

"I want you to see a doctor. I don't like it that you're having pains. Where is the hospital?"

She told him, but added, "I'm a doctor." She preferred going to her ob-gyn without him. And she would, as soon as she dropped him off at the resort.

"I'm taking you to the hospital. Then, when the royal physician gets here, he'll check you, too, just to be safe."

"I can take myself."

He looked over, holding her gaze for a long second. "Why do you insist on fighting me at every turn, even when what I propose is to your benefit?"

"Because if I didn't, you would take over. You would want to help me with everything."

"Why do you fear that?"

"Because I would come to depend on you. Little by little, I would change. I wouldn't be the independent woman that I am now. Then, when I was weak, you would lose interest and leave me, and I would be so dependent by then that I wouldn't be able to handle it."

"Was that your mother's story?"

She hated that he got right to the truth. She didn't want to think about her mother right now. She looked down at her lap. "Yes, it was. And I'm not going to repeat it."

"You won't."

She looked back at him. "How do you know?"

"You are the strongest woman I know, bar none, and believe me when I say this, since my sister Saida is really something. She's one big royal headache." He gave a brief sigh. "You took care of your dying father. You have single-handedly kept me alive for the past month. You've been on the run with me for the past day, dodging bullets while nine-months pregnant. Not only are you fiercely independent, but you're brave. Nothing scares you."

"*Everything* scares me," she admitted for the first time, surprising herself.

As much as she wanted to be strong and independent, deep down she was scared of living the rest of her life alone, scared of raising her son alone, scared of what would happen if all she could give him wasn't enough. What did she know about being a mother? Her own mother had never been around, never been available.

"Fine, you're scared sometimes. But you don't let that stop you. That's true courage."

The honest admiration in his voice made her heart turn over in her chest.

He took the street on their right and she saw the hospital was at the corner. He pulled into the underground parking and went all the way to the lowest level, parked in a far spot, but didn't get out.

He took her hand and kept it enveloped in his. "Do you think me a weak man?"

She nearly laughed. The words *weak* and *Amir* didn't belong on the same page. "Hardly."

That seemed to please him. "Yet I depended on you like a small babe for weeks. I needed you. I need you still. It would be all right if we needed each other, don't you think?"

The image was tempting, but him needing her for anything, now that he was recovered, was difficult to believe. "You would rule me."

"We would rule our country together. Marriage is a partnership, not a dictatorship."

"That's what you say now," she replied, fighting back, weaker than she wanted to be. He was so earnest, she could almost believe him.

He went quiet for a few long seconds, watching her closely. Then he asked with all seriousness, "Do you love another? I ask only that you answer this one question honestly."

"There's no one else."

Her immediate, sure response seemed to please him thoroughly.

"But I'm not in love with you, either," she added quickly. "And you're not in love with me. Wouldn't you want that in your marriage? A whole life is a very long time to spend with a person you weren't meant to be with."

He paused, giving himself time to think it over, and she liked that. He wasn't mindlessly pushing his agenda on her. He listened to what she had to say and was carefully weighing it.

The overhead lights cast his regal features in a glow. "Love will come. I respect you and admire you for who you are. If you can accept me for who I am, that is not a bad starting point."

His dark gaze enveloped her, mesmerized her. The knowledge that he saw her differently than anyone else, differently even than she saw herself, that he thought her somehow special, was intoxicating, even without a heated declaration of love.

Vanity, she told herself. *Nothing but vanity.*

But...

Respect and admiration. A marriage could be built on worse things. His words held truth, even if she wasn't ready to accept that truth yet.

She felt a small bond form between them as he held her hand, strengthening the one that had already existed, the bond of their baby. A bond that, she understood now, was much stronger than she had thought. She would have to plan for that, accommodate it.

"Isabelle?" His gaze heated, his head tilting toward hers.

Her lips tingled at the thought of another kiss. Leaning into his waiting strength was tempting. It would have been too easy. So she made sure she didn't. She pulled away. "We better get going."

Chapter Six

He hated the sight of her hooked to machines. He would have much rather faced enemy fire than stand helplessly by her side, not knowing what to do to make her better. She claimed all the pain was gone, but then why were those machines beeping?

Amir had always enjoyed good health, could not recall ever spending time in a hospital. Dumont General left him with a sense of unease, even if Isabelle's doctor appeared competent enough. Because of that, he'd decided to allow him to continue her care until the royal physician could take over.

He didn't like it, but he would allow it. He was a reasonable man. He couldn't fathom why Isabelle would call him stubborn. Nobody had ever referred to him that way before. Maybe Saida, his little sister, once or twice. Both women were wrong, of course. He was decisive and firm in his opinions—both qualities an asset in a ruler.

He crossed his arms in front of him, his shoulders growing more tense with every passing minute as he waited for the doctor to say something.

"Looks like what we have here is some Braxton Hicks. Practice contractions." The man read from the display on the machine that Isabelle had been hooked up to for the past hour. He was older, probably close to retirement, with sharp eyes but a kind voice, reminding Amir of his father's favorite advisor.

"I'm going to order an ultrasound, just in case," the man told Isabelle.

Didn't seem like Isabelle was going into labor immediately. And whatever practice contractions were, they didn't sound life-threatening. Amir relaxed a little. He wanted to take her home for the baby's birth. He needed time. He just found out yesterday that he was going to be a father. He could use a day or two to prepare before meeting his son.

"I'll be coming along." He wasn't going to let her out of his sight.

"No need to go anywhere. I'll have a machine brought in here. Let me quickly check her for dilation first. Just to be safe."

Amir did step outside for that, scanned the hallway for anyone suspicious who might have followed them here. When he didn't find anything out of the ordinary, he strode to the end of the hall and used the pay phone to call Efraim. He had seen the phone earlier, but had refused to leave Isabelle's side until he knew that whatever was causing her pain wasn't serious.

"I'm coming to the resort and I'm bringing someone with me."

"Are you joking?" Efraim wanted to know on the other end. "All this time, we've been worried about you, investigated your disappearance, feared that you were dead, and you were shacked up with a woman? Of all the crazy, irresponsible things you've ever done—"

"The circumstances—"

"There are always circumstances with you when there is a beautiful woman involved," Efraim said, exasperated. "And here I was, thinking how you'd matured lately. Who is she? Another actress?"

"That was before."

"When you were the Black Sheep Sheik?"

He was starting to get annoyed. "A friend wouldn't call me that." Bad enough that the tabloids had tagged him with the infernal nickname. He had a feeling that he could live a lifetime with exemplary discipline and still not be rid of it.

"A friend wouldn't take off and leave the summit hanging by a thread for a set of pretty eyes and a pair of nice legs."

"I did no such thing." He tried to keep his voice down but only partially succeeded.

"She doesn't have pretty eyes and nice legs?"

He ground his teeth.

"I thought so." Efraim was infuriatingly smug.

Time to change the subject. "I heard you had trouble at the resort."

"Not a subject for the phone," his friend said, now somber. "I'll fill you in when you get here.

Don't talk to anyone else in the meanwhile. Not your security, not even the local police."

"I see." Isabelle had mentioned trouble with the local police, and his secretary had told him about Fahad. He'd been hoping that maybe they were wrong, but it didn't look like that was the case. Nor did it make much sense.

If his security was involved, which Fahad's betrayal indicated, that meant the threat came from home. But if the local police could not be trusted, that would mean his enemies were from here, from the United States. He knew precious little, and the information he had was conflicting. The sooner he got to the resort and heard the details, the better. The more he knew, the better he could protect Isabelle.

"Are you going to tell me what kept you so busy that you couldn't call us before now?" Efraim drilled him. "Was it this woman? You never lost your head like this, Amir. Not to the point of forgetting your responsibilities. I'm worried about you." His voice was uncharacteristically tight.

"And angry." As if Isabelle being angry at him wasn't enough.

"Yes. Things have been…difficult here. For all of us. Also, there've been other, personal changes…. Never mind that now. I can tell you later."

"And I'll explain everything when I see you." Right now, he wanted to be back with Isabelle. But he did have one more question. "Are you and the others safe?"

"Probably not, but we're holding up our end. Tell me where you are, and we'll come and get you."

"No." They would only draw attention. The safest thing was for him to take Isabelle to the resort himself, sneaking in unseen. "Have you heard from my royal physician?"

"Should we have?"

"He'll be arriving later today."

"Are you hurt?"

"I need to go." He didn't want to miss anything important back in the examining room, so he hung up the phone, then headed back to Isabelle and their baby.

"ARE YOU SURE you can handle it this time?" the caller asked darkly.

"Yes, sir. We have their car tagged. All we have to do is follow the signal."

"Where is he now?"

"Dumont General."

"Busy place." He wanted results, not publicity.

"We have a plan," the man said proudly. "We can take him with minimum exposure."

They'd said that before. He was seriously beginning to doubt the local crew he had recruited. "How about a plan B?"

Silence on the other end.

He sighed. Idiots, down to the last of them. "See that the chase ends this time. I don't handle disappointment well." A clear warning.

"Yes, sir."

AMIR STRODE BACK into the examining room and ran his disjointed theories about the attacks through his mind while the doctor squeezed some bluish jelly on Isabelle's belly, then began the ultrasound. A shapeless blob twisted on the black-and-white screen. Fuzzy. Then two blobs, one bigger, one smaller.

Her doctor's opinion aside, the royal physician was going to check her out the second they were all at the resort. And as soon as he pronounced Isabelle fit to fly, she would be on a plane to Jamala, away from all danger. Not that he had a firm grip on where that danger was coming from, or who exactly wanted him dead. Which drove him crazy.

He was a warrior at heart. He wanted a clear-cut enemy he could fight. He needed a target to direct his anger against. He needed to do something other than escape and evade, which went against his basic personality.

"There. Already positioned with the head down. Good strong heartbeat." The doctor was smiling.

But Amir could barely hear the words. The world stopped spinning all of a sudden. Because he could make out the shape of a baby's head at last. The eyes, the lips, the mouth, the chin. *His* chin! That was the Khalid chin for certain.

He wasn't prepared for the emotions that flooded him, bowled him over where he stood. Until now, the baby inside Isabelle had been a concept, some little boy who would be his heir one day, would take over the country in the distant future. The uppermost emotions he'd felt were possessiveness and protectiveness. But now came love, an instant, forever kind of love that took the breath right out of his chest.

His son.

The two short words were suddenly full of meaning. He looked at Isabelle, wanting to know if she understood what an utter miracle this was, truly felt the significance of it. Her blue eyes swam with tears as they met his.

"Textbook perfect," the doctor was saying. "You're pretty close. From now on, I'd like to see you every day if you can come in."

"I will. I'm ready for this. Carrying this little peanut is backbreaking work. Not that I'm complaining." She turned to smile at the screen, blinking hard a couple of times. "But he can come whenever he wants. Thank you, Dr. Szunoman."

"I'll let you get dressed. See you tomorrow then. Same time would be good for me. I'll be on call for the next two days." The doctor wiped off her belly, then congratulated Amir on his way out, but Amir's eyes were still on the monitor.

"That's my son."

Isabelle tugged her shirt down and sat up, rolling her eyes, blinking away her tears. "Our son. I think I had a little something to do with this pregnancy."

He caught her up in a hug and swung her around, unable to stop grinning. "My son and my wife." He sure hadn't expected that when he'd come back to Wyoming. He wasn't sure if he deserved being so richly blessed.

"Amir." Her tone held as much warning as a Wild West gunslinger's as she pushed against him with determination. "No."

He set her down but kept his arms around her. "Give me one good reason why not. You can trust me. I will take care of you," he said before he could stop himself, knowing immediately that he'd said the wrong thing. It was the taking care of part that she hated and feared the most. "Or I'll ignore you," he offered. "I promise to be too busy taking care of the country to take care of you properly."

She ignored that last bit, not even bothering to point out how badly he was faking. "You can't take care of me. Nobody can take care of me. I have to take care of myself. I'm not going to end up like my mother."

He stepped away from her, his own frustration rising. She was carrying his child. He wanted to marry her. Why was she resisting? "What does this have to do with your mother? What did your father do to her?"

"It wasn't my father." She walked out of the room and down the hallway. "My mother went from, well, trailer trash to one of the first women golf champions, always trying to get someone to take care of her on the way. First my father…" Her voice faltered. "Marrying a doctor at eighteen was a big deal to her. Like a prize or something. He was another one of her trophies."

He stopped her, turned her to him, then reached out to push a few stray locks of hair back from her beautiful face. "Marrying a doctor is not a crime, Isabelle. In fact, a lot of women out there wouldn't mind being married to a sheik, either."

She swatted his hand away. "She wasn't happy with him for long. After I was born, she moved on to her manager. Then her sponsor. She was always looking for the next more powerful man who could take her even higher. They used her, then cast her aside. Then... Never mind. We should be going." She looked away and began walking toward the elevators.

Sounded like her mother had been taken advantage of sexually by these powerful men in her life. And now Isabelle didn't trust men in power. His hands fisted as he followed her. "Then?"

"She started drinking and doing performance-enhancing drugs and her career disappeared. Her liver gave out at the end."

They stopped in front of the elevators.

He took her hand and wouldn't let her pull away. "You're not your mother."

"No." She gave a sour laugh. "She used people and allowed them to use her. I try so hard not to be like her that I make even worse mistakes."

He lifted her chin so he could look into her amazing blue eyes. Her soft black hair framed her face. He had known his share of beautiful women. She was the most beautiful of all. Of course, he could be biased. But even if she wasn't the most beautiful woman he'd ever met, she certainly was the one from whom he couldn't look away. "This is not a mistake."

"I don't let anyone close, for fear of starting to depend on them too much. I work too hard at the hospital to ensure I'll never have to depend on anyone. The first man I let near me in years was a complete stranger at a masquerade ball, a man whose name I didn't ask to make sure there could be no possible entanglements. And now here we are." She tugged her hand out of his.

She went on. "I don't regret being pregnant. But I wasn't looking for commitment. I wasn't looking for any of this. We used protection."

And this time he let her go. "I see."

She viewed a relationship with him as some sort of prison. The thought brought a strange tightness to his chest. As a very eligible prince, he hadn't experienced too much rejection. His usual response to failure was to try harder, but pushing her now didn't seem the right thing. If she didn't want him, he couldn't force himself on her. He did care about her happiness. He would not be the source of her misery. "We'll talk about this some more at another time."

"I've been talking." She stepped onto the elevator. "I can talk all I want, but will you listen?"

That she was right stung. He hadn't been listening very well until now. He hadn't realized how strongly she felt about her independence until he'd heard her mother's story. "I will," he promised as the metal doors closed behind them.

She shook her head, a wry smile on her lips. "You have no idea how wretched saying that made you look."

"Sheiks don't look wretched. Noble. Aristocratic. Devilishly handsome. Those are the usual adjectives, I believe." He wanted to make her laugh.

She rolled her eyes, the smile growing a little. "Whatever."

Why was it so hard for them to make each other understand? "The strange thing is, even though I'm a sheik, you…make me feel like an ordinary man." She'd said she wanted an ordinary man, if any. Maybe they were going in the right direction.

She tilted her head. "Is that a bad thing?"

"Probably not. I suppose it's a learning experience. I'm not always certain what to do with the way you respond to me."

"You mean you don't know how to handle it when your every word isn't taken as a command?"

He flashed her a dark glare.

"I'm guessing you would know better how to react if I just fell at your feet and told you to do with me as you wish."

He brightened up instantly. They were on the same page at last. "Yes."

"Fat chance." She sneered.

He went back to glaring, but not really feeling it. "You've been mocking me again."

"Is that a hanging offense in Jamala? If it is, I better not go there."

"It should be," he said, but he was laughing under

his breath. She really was amazing, could frustrate and make him laugh at the same time. She had a talent for reaching his emotions on multiple levels.

"Yes, O powerful sheik." Her smile now bloomed wide on her full lips. Obviously, she was enjoying making fun of him. Seeing him unsettled seemed to give her pleasure. Heaven help him.

He wished for only one pleasure himself—the pleasure of kissing that mocking smile off her lips, the pleasure of seeing her in his bed. *Soon,* he promised himself. "We will discuss the matter of our relationship seriously. We will have time when we're safe at the resort."

She watched him for a long moment. "You want serious? All right, answer a single question honestly. Did you come to Wyoming with the intent of marrying me? Or did you have me tracked down for another roll in the hay?" She looked him squarely in the eyes, her smile gone.

"Back then—"

"Yes or no," she demanded.

"No."

"Which means you only want to marry me now because of the baby. We don't do that here. Women can support themselves."

"The baby and you are my responsibility. I admit, I have not been the most responsible person all my life." In fact, he'd been known for some wild partying and reckless behavior. "But once I do take responsibility for something, I honor my commitments."

"That's just it, don't you see?" she said softly. "I don't want to be another responsibility that has been foisted upon you. I don't want to be the woman you grow to resent little by little for putting you in chains. It would kill the soul right out of us if we had to live like that, together for all the wrong reasons, day after day."

There was a communication gap between them. Making her understand him was vital. He needed to figure out how to convince her, and in order to do that, he needed to spend more time with her.

"Will you come to the resort with me? The rest of the royals are there with whatever trustworthy security we have left. I wish to see you safe. You've been seen with me a number of times. Your car has been seen. They have your license-plate number. By now they know where you work, where you live."

Still, she thought about it way too long. Then, at last, her hand came to rest on her belly. "All right. I'll stay at the resort until it's time for me to have the baby."

Good. An excellent first step.

They exited the elevator in silence. He kept in front of her while he looked around. Nothing suspicious in the underground parking garage that he could see, and he did peer hard into every shadowed corner. Neon lights flickered above, in a neat row in the middle.

"What will your family think of this? I mean about the baby," she asked out of the blue. "I know absolutely nothing about your family. What will your parents say? You said before that you had a sister and a half brother." She drew her delicate eyebrows together. "That would have been a good time to mention that you were all royalty."

"Not all, technically. My half brother lives right around here." Finding him had been the reason for his first trip to Wyoming all those months ago. "Our parents are gone now. My father had a secret indiscretion many years ago. Wade was never formally acknowledged. My sister Saida doesn't even know about him." He wanted to talk to Wade again and bring the family together at last. As soon as Isabelle was safe.

"You mean royal families aren't perfect, either?"

"Don't you read tabloids?"

"If I ever get a chance to sit down at the hospital, I'm lucky to get through the contents page of the *New England Journal of Medicine.* People vastly overestimate the amount of time most doctors have for leisure activities."

He took her hand as they walked through the deserted, exhaust-smelling lot. He had chosen the lower, emptier level on purpose. His picture had been on the news. He didn't want anyone to recognize him. He had a feeling Isabelle's doctor had, but she had a longtime friendship with the man through the hospital, so Amir didn't think he had anything to worry about from that corner.

They were about halfway to Isabelle's car when the first shot rang out. And he couldn't knock Isabelle to the ground and throw himself on top of her, for fear of hurting her or the baby.

He rushed her into the cover of a cement support post instead, positioning her between the post and himself to make sure she was protected from two sides. Not enough, but something. His hands went to his waist, where he often wore a holstered weapon when he thought he might be entering a dangerous situation. But this time, of course, he had nothing.

The enemy's gun fell silent. The man was probably moving closer, trying to find a more vulnerable angle. He wasn't going to have too difficult a time. They were sitting ducks here.

The distraction of another car pulling into the parking area would have been welcome, but the place was quiet, nobody coming. Somebody would, sooner or later, but they didn't have too long to wait. The second the shooter found them, the game would be over.

"Who are these people?" Desperation thickened Isabelle's voice.

"I don't know. But when I find out, I promise you, there'll be hell to pay." He searched for a weapon, spotted a fire extinguisher on the far wall, impossible to reach.

Isabelle was searching, too, her gaze darting from car to car. "Where do we hide?"

His muscles tightened. He wanted to reassure her, but he had little good news to give. "No place to hide here. I'm sorry."

Her SUV was in a clear line of sight, most of the

way protected by the emergency staircase. "We will run for it," he told her. "Zigzag. Between here and there, take every available cover. No matter what anyone says or does, no matter what happens to me, you just keep going. I need you to promise me that."

"It's impossible." She looked pale and worried, her eyes large in her face.

"Not nearly. Reminds me of running with the bulls in Spain." He made his tone lighter for her sake, wanting to erase the fear from her eyes. "I'll tell you about the good old days when we get out of here."

"You didn't run with the bulls."

"Seven times," he told her proudly. "Now!"

They dashed forward, stopping in the cover of an enormous pickup truck. He normally sneered at giant American monstrosities, but now he was grateful for the size. Cars in his country were much smaller; the roads narrower. The original road system had been built for donkey-cart traffic.

"What about security?" Isabelle was asking him in a low whisper.

"I don't know if I can trust my security," he told her morosely.

"I mean in Spain. How could they let you risk your life like that?"

Either she was the coolest person under pressure, or she was trying to distract herself from the threat of imminent death so she could function.

"I left my security at the hotel. Nobody knew who I was."

They dashed another ten yards, then stopped by the next support column and crouched at its base. Too slow. Only luck saved them. He was still too damned weak. A week from now, he could probably take on the bastard. Take him on and rip his heart out for putting Isabelle in danger.

As it was, if he wasn't careful, he wasn't going to live to see next week.

"I thought sheiks were supposed to be responsible and all that. What was that embracing responsibility speech you gave me before? The whole 'being the father of your nation' thing?"

"I haven't run with the bulls since I took the throne." Not that anybody appreciated that or any of the other sacrifices he'd made. Everybody took his complete lifestyle change for granted.

And his life was about to change again. Completely. Yet, this time, he didn't feel a single spark of resentment. He was looking forward to this twist. *Then do what you have to so you live that long,* he told himself as he inspected their surroundings.

They had only another five yards separating them from Isabelle's car, but they would have to come out into the open to close that distance. He scanned the area again, looking for another alternative and not finding any.

"Get your keys out."

She did so immediately.

"I'll distract them. You run to the car and drive

out of here as fast as you can. Without looking back, without a moment of hesitation. They're after me. They will leave you alone. Don't stop until you're someplace safe."

Her chin came up, and he knew what was coming before she said the words. There was something tragically heroic about her, in the fire in her blue eyes.

"I'm not leaving you in here with some armed madman. I don't care if you've run with the bulls, wild elephants or a yeti."

He didn't have time to argue with her. He raked his brain for a compromise, aware that with every second they wasted hesitating, the shooter was creeping closer and closer to them.

"You can't move as fast as I can," he pointed out. "I'll run for the elevators and keep in cover. I'll meet you at the front entrance of the hospital. We'll be safe there. There's security in the lobby."

"What if they catch you?"

"They won't. It's not the first tight spot I've been in in my life, Isabelle. I know what to do. I'll be fine."

"You're still recovering."

"I only have to make it to the elevators. It's a very short sprint."

She looked like she was going to argue with him, but in the end, she didn't.

"Be safe," she told him, then ran for it, keys in one hand, the other resting protectively over her belly.

He sprung up at the same time, drawing attention to himself.

A third of the way there.

A shot rang out, the bullet hitting the tailgate of the pickup in front of him.

Halfway there.

The next bullet hit the cement at his feet.

Almost there.

But before his finger reached the call button, the third bullet mercilessly slammed into him, knocking him to the ground, searing his body with pain.

Chapter Seven

Amir was hit.

Isabelle saw him jerk as his body absorbed the impact of the bullet. Then she could no longer see him as he fell. The shooter knew he had him and stepped out into the open, moving in for the kill.

"Stop!" She yanked her black mini-umbrella from her purse and angled her body to keep her shaky hands in the shadow, hoping like hell she looked armed and dangerous.

She had no idea what on earth she was doing. All she knew was that she couldn't let Amir die here.

"Stop right there, or I'll shoot," she ordered in her toughest tone, the one she normally reserved for dressing down unruly residents at the hospital. Or patients she caught eating double cheeseburgers the night before surgery.

Then two things happened at the same time: the man turned his back to Amir and moved toward her, and a car entered the parking lot, its headlights hitting the umbrella, ending the illusion that she was holding a gun.

Blazing buzzards.

The attacker was closer to her than to Amir. In a few steps he was by her side, swearing, yanking her between two minivans and out of sight of the approaching car.

A rough-palmed hand clamped over her mouth before she could call out for help. In seconds they were at the black van parked in the back; then the side door opened and hands reached out of the darkness, pulled her up and in.

She kept her hands around her belly to protect the baby. Two men were in the back, at least one up front, driving. She could see only shapes, very little light filtering through the small window that was the only connection between the back of the van and the cab.

The men stayed silent while the vehicle sped out of the parking garage, tires squealing. She stayed down and remained still, giving them no reason whatsoever to get rough with her. Amir was her only thought. Let him be all right. Let him find her.

Then she realized that she still had her key ring hooked around her thumb. Without her car, Amir couldn't follow the van, even if he wasn't seriously injured. And if he was? She had to get back to him.

Whatever cool and calm she'd been faking fled in an instant. Panic set in. Shivering fear.

"Please let me go. Please. I'm going to have a baby soon—"

One man taped her hands together in front of her; another taped her mouth shut, effectively ending her begging.

AMIR RAN AFTER the van for as long as he could. Not nearly long enough. He gasped for air, ignoring the spasms in his side, the muscle pain in his legs, the pain of the bullet in his shoulder. He cursed the weak physical condition he was in after lying in bed for a month. But he kept moving even as he did that. Pushed around the bend. Jumped to the side when he was almost hit by a pickup. He didn't bother to stop for the honking driver. He kept running up the parking ramp to street level.

"Isabelle!"

When he knew without a doubt that he wasn't going to catch up with them, when he lost sight of the van down the boulevard, he dragged his wheezing self back to the hospital. He grabbed a soiled hospital gown from a temporarily abandoned cart by the employee entrance and draped it over his bloody shoulder.

The bullet had gone straight through, as far as he could tell. He didn't have time to worry about the injury at the moment. He strode to the main entrance and straight to the nearest pay phone, then called the resort.

"I need a car sent to the Dumont hospital for me. Immediately."

Efraim didn't ask questions; even as Amir was

hanging up the phone, his friend was barking orders on the other end.

The car was there in twenty minutes, along with two bodyguards. Another twenty minutes and they were pulling into the resort. Stefan, Efraim and Antoine were waiting for him in Stefan's suite. With a surprise.

Darek, prince of Saruk, was with them.

Amir greeted him first. "What are you doing here?" His country wasn't part of COIN.

Darek embraced him as if they were true brothers. "I came to help."

The royal physician came through the door, looking bleary-eyed. "I flew all night to get here. Would you please sit, Your Highness?" He immediately saw to the wound.

His friend Sebastian, prince of Barajas, came in behind him. "I came as soon as I heard. We were on the same flight." He greeted Amir first, then the others.

"Where have you been?" Efraim sat on a chair by Amir's side. "Where is this mystery woman you were supposed to bring?"

"When did you get hurt?" Stefan took in the wound and shook his head.

"Who else knows that you're alive?"

"Why didn't you call before?"

Amir cut off any further questions with a gesture of his hand. "I was in a coma from the explosion until yesterday evening. None of that is important now. The most important thing is that the mother of my son was kidnapped from the hospital. I need to find her."

A silent hush fell over the room. They all stared.

"You want me to set up a press conference to announce your safe return?" Stefan asked. "The media has finally decamped. They had this place swamped for a while after you went missing. I'm sure news of you can bring them back in a hurry."

"Not until we have Isabelle back."

"You have a son?" Efraim asked.

"He'll be born in a few days. I met Isabelle the last time I was here. Then I was on my way to see her again the night the limousine was blown up." He summed up the rest in as few sentences as he could; then it was his turn to question the others. "What have you found out about the explosion?"

He sat slack-jawed when they were finished. "The Russian mob?"

Stefan's lips narrowed. "They were hired men. We haven't been able to figure out who was behind them. We had…some distractions," he admitted.

"And Fahad?"

"That was the biggest shock." Efraim shook his head, sorrow and anger clear in his dark eyes. Fahad was his cousin.

"Saida will be disappointed," Amir muttered to himself, thanking the heavens that his sister was safe and far away from here. She had a lot of respect for Fahad and, Amir thought, perhaps even a schoolgirl's crush on the man when she was younger.

"Saida came here when she found out that you disappeared. She is getting married," Efraim said cautiously.

Amir's head whipped up. He pinned his best friend with a killer look. "I don't remember anyone asking my permission."

"Not me." Efraim raised his hands with haste. "It seems she's become enamored with the local sheriff."

"Is she at the resort?"

"She had to fly back to Jamala for a few days to smooth some ruffled feathers. Your continued absence… Anyhow, she's grown into quite the diplomat. Nasir is with her for protection. She'll be back on Monday. She's been calling. She wants you to call her as soon as you have a minute."

Probably to ask his permission to marry. Like hell was some Wyoming wild man going to marry his little sister. In case they'd all forgotten, she was a princess.

"Jake Wolf is on his way, actually. You can sort that out with him when he gets here." Efraim was grinning in anticipation.

"The least I would have expected from my friends is to guard my sister's honor while I was incapacitated." They were going to have more words about that later. "I thought the police weren't to be trusted."

"That's the previous sheriff and his cronies," Sebastian said. "Mr. Wolf seems like a decent man. He saved Saida's life."

Amir jumped up, ignoring the doctor's yelp. The man had been about to sew his wound together. "Saida was in danger?"

"She insisted on being involved with the investigation into your disappearance. There was no holding her back." Antoine hung his head, as if embarrassed that the four of them couldn't control one woman.

Knowing his little sister, Amir couldn't truly blame them. She was another one of those independent sorts, like Isabelle. He didn't understand today's women. His mother had always been the very picture of matrimonial obedience. A thought he didn't have time to ponder at the moment. He sat back down and let the doctor take over again. "But she's safe now?"

Efraim nodded. "Absolutely, yes."

"Actually, hers might not be the only upcoming royal wedding," Sebastian said with a sheepish expression on his face.

Amir's eyebrows slid up. "What are you talking about?"

"You missed an eventful month." Stefan shrugged. "We all sort of, well, met our matches one way or the other."

He took a few seconds to process that. "I was missing in action and you took time for romance?" He didn't know whether to feel insulted or to laugh. They'd always been confirmed bachelors, the five of them.

"Exactly why I came over," Darek teased. "Someone had to keep a straight head on his shoulders."

"Danger and romance are not as incompatible as one would think," Sebastian declared, waxing philosophical.

And Amir couldn't contradict that. His connection with Isabelle had only grown through the danger they'd faced together. And she was still in danger, in more danger now than she had ever been. "Hurry up," he snapped at the doctor.

"All done, sir," the royal physician assured him, having bandaged him in the meanwhile. "The bullet went straight through. It shouldn't get infected. All you need is rest. Is there anything else you require?"

"I didn't bring you here for myself," he told the man, his patience on its last leg, frustration and worry over Isabelle tightening his muscles. "You will be attending to my future wife as soon as we recover her."

Antoine brought over a plate of food without remarking on Amir's paleness or the weight he'd lost, which he appreciated. Just now he didn't want to dwell on his weakness.

"Where do you think they took her?" Antoine asked.

"I don't know." He didn't feel like eating. He chose what looked like a turkey sandwich, anyway, and took a healthy bite. He needed to regain his strength. "But I have the license-plate number of the van."

"Good. Then we'll start with that." A man who

looked at least partially Native American came through the door, a sheriff's star on his shirt.

That had to be Jake Wolf, the bastard who had seduced Saida. Amir put down the sandwich and stood. Damn it all that he still didn't have a gun, while the sheriff was armed. He hadn't been in a good mood to begin with, but Wolf's cheerful face rubbed him just the wrong way. He opened his mouth to rip into him, but Wolf spoke first.

"Sheik Amir, I'm Jake Wolf, sheriff of Dumont County. I would like to ask you for the honor of your sister's hand in marriage."

That gave him pause. All right, so maybe he had *some* manners and his intentions were possibly honorable.

"I will answer that request after I've had a chance to converse with Saida."

"Fair enough," the man said easily, looking like a besotted fool who was so far gone in love he actually didn't think he had anything to fear from the Black Sheep Sheik. "What do we know?"

Amir rattled off the letters and numbers of the license-plate number, and Wolf called it in. They had an address within thirty seconds.

Then there was a fight over who should go. All the royals insisted, including Darek. In the end, it was agreed that having them out in public would only complicate things and might put Isabelle in even more danger.

"You all stay. I'll go with my most trusted men." Wolf headed for the door.

Amir grabbed a gun from the table and followed.

Wolf, oblivious to danger, blocked his way. "You should stay, Sheik Amir."

"Can you envision a situation, Mr. Wolf," Amir asked in a tone of clear warning, "in which my sister was in trouble and you would stay home while others went off to rescue her?"

The sheriff's lips narrowed; his shoulders went still and stiff. Then he went through the door without another word of protest, and Amir followed him. Wolf was calling in reinforcements on the way.

Amir prayed they wouldn't be too late.

"WE'LL BE FINE." Isabelle placed her hand on her belly. "I'm not going to let anything bad happen to either of us. By hook or crook, whatever it takes. You have to trust me on this. Did I tell you that Wyoming law requires that children believe their mother?"

She was locked in an abandoned basement office. She had no idea where. The van had no windows in the back, and they hadn't let her out until the garage door had been closed behind them. All she'd seen was a short hallway with a closed door at the end and the basement door to the left. They'd gone down one flight of rickety wooden steps to an unfinished space, save the small, windowless office in the corner. At least it had an attached powder room that housed a cracked toilet and a lime-scale-covered sink.

Her back was killing her. She sat on the dusty

chair, contemplating lying down on the dirty floor. The baby seemed to gain weight every day, her belly putting more and more strain on her spine. Her legs were a little swollen, but nothing serious, a normal part of this stage of pregnancy. Her cramps had stopped, which was a huge relief. She didn't want to give birth in this godforsaken place.

"Remember how I said this morning that you could come anytime now?" she asked her son. "On second thought, I'd really appreciate another week."

She would have appreciated a host of other things as well, like knowing what had happened to Amir, if he'd made it. He'd gone down. How bad was his injury?

She looked around once again, hoping to spot something this time that might help her open the door. They'd taken her purse and car keys. She was still wearing the cowboy shirt over her maternity dress, the cowboy boots still on her feet.

She could probably kick the door open—she had serious weight to put behind the kick—but that would be heard. She needed a quieter method. Amir might have had an idea if he were here. Too late, she was beginning to appreciate him and the concept of teamwork. Right now, actually, it wouldn't be all that bad if somebody had her back.

Voices filtered through the heating vent: men were speaking, but not loudly enough for her to make out the words. She stared at the grate wistfully. Spies and thieves crawled through industrial-size vents all the time in the movies. But these ducts were way too small for that, especially with her current figure. Not to mention she would need a crane to lift her to the ceiling.

Right here was the reason why action flicks rarely featured pregnant women. No movies called *The Gestating Spy* or *Mission: Maternity* ever topped the box office.

This battle clearly wasn't going to be won on physical ability. *Think.* She turned to the desk and went through the drawers again one by one. Didn't find as much as a paper clip. Whoever owned the house might be a murderous bastard, but he sure was tidy.

She looked around again. There had to be something she wasn't seeing. There had to be a way out of here—

Something she wasn't seeing. Her hands flew to her ears and she just about ripped out her new earrings. She straightened the hypoallergenic surgical steel hoops as best she could and headed for the door. Even the baby kicked in excitement. The lock wasn't complicated—it was an average double-sided lock they sold at The Home Depot. Figuring out how to bend the metal just right was the trick. Good thing she had clever surgeon fingers.

She inserted the bent thicker end of one earring and tried to manipulate the tumblers. Something clicked, but the door wouldn't open. Footsteps sounded upstairs. She pushed harder. Too hard. She broke her makeshift pick. She tossed it on the floor and bent the other earring into a zigzag shape, tried the lock again.

"Come on, come on. Work, please."

And as if that had been all the encouragement the door had been waiting for, the lock popped again, opening this time.

She peeked out. Couldn't see anyone in the basement. Couldn't see a direct exit to the outside, either. She kept close to the wall and tiptoed to the stairs, listened. Nothing. If there was anyone at the top of the stairs, he was staying silent.

She put her foot on the first step, then held her breath when it creaked. Still no sound from above. She made her way up step by step, barely daring to breathe on the way, wishing that Amir was here with her. And not caring whether that made her less self-reliant or weak.

The next door blocked her way. Her hand shook as she put it on the knob. Twisted the metal. It didn't give. She could have cried when she realized this door was locked as well. She'd left her earring in the previous door. Should have thought of that. She tried the knob again. Definitely locked. Which meant that she had to sneak back down for her makeshift lock pick, then up again, risking noise and the possibility of being discovered.

By the time she made that nerve-racking trip and was ready to put the zigzag-shaped piece of metal to use, her forehead was beaded with sweat.

She tried to be careful, but this lock was as tough as the first. The tip of her pick broke off within seconds. "Okay, don't do this. Just work. Please," she whispered, using the piece she had left. And the lock clicked open at last, at the same time as the pick snapped in half. She waited for her heart to slow before she opened the door a crack.

The door to the garage she'd come through earlier was closed, but the door that led to the rest of the house was open. The men were arguing about money, although she couldn't see any of them, just an empty hallway with peeling wallpaper.

She waited, trying to decide what to do, nearly jumping out of her skin from nerves every time someone raised his voice. They were out of her line of sight for the moment, but who knew how quickly that would change once she stepped out into the hallway? Still, she had no choice but to try. She flattened herself against the wall, hoping her belly wasn't sticking out too far. *Okay, kiddo, pull your legs in.*

She didn't dare look back as she inched forward. Then she was at the door that led to the garage. If it was locked, she was trapped. She had nothing left to open another lock with.

She put her hand on the knob and prayed. It turned smoothly under her hand. Whoever had kidnapped her must have felt safe in this place, having no concern about being discovered and busted in on.

She pushed against the door, cringed at the soft creak. Stopped and waited. Nobody came.

In seconds she was in the garage. The only exit

was the automatic garage door. If she opened that, the men inside would hear for sure. They would rush out, and she wasn't going to win a footrace with this belly.

She moved to the van and glanced in through the window. The keys dangled in the ignition.

"We are so out of here," she told her son. "You just watch your mother."

"Cops are on the way."

"We didn't even deliver the ransom note yet." The man swore to himself. He didn't want to end up like the previous team leader. The money was good, but not enough to die for.

"Get out. Take her with you. Alive."

"Ain't she supposed to be disposable?"

"Not until we have the sheik."

He didn't ask questions. *Keep your head down and collect the money*—that was the game he played.

THEY HAD THE house surrounded. Amir squatted behind a row of boxwood bushes across the road in a neighbor's yard—waiting for the signal.

"We go in. You observe," Wolf was saying next to him, his tone all business. "Maybe take this time to give Wade Freeman a call. He's been checking in with me every couple of days for news of you. He'd been concerned." Wolf's tone said he knew of the secret brotherly connection.

"Who else knows?" Introducing his long-lost half

brother to the public had to be done delicately. His existence was going to bring about some political complications no doubt.

"Only Saida." He shifted. "It's time. You sit tight."

"I'm going in."

"With all due respect, Sheik Amir, you're not."

He fixed the man with his most authoritative glare. "You cannot stop me."

"I can handcuff you to the mailbox."

"And marry my sister?" He gave the guy a level look.

Wolf shot his own level look back. "Are you blackmailing a sheriff?"

"A simple conversation between potential family members."

"I cannot officially authorize a civilian joining a takedown." Wolf looked at the house. "Wait at least a minute before you follow me, despite an express order to stay here."

Amir was starting to like the man. He had a backbone and a sense of humor. Of course, he should have known that. Saida couldn't abide weaklings. But before he could give more thought to his sister's chosen mate, the sheriff gave the signal and rushed forward in a crouch, along with the rest of his men, who were closing in on the disheveled rancher from every direction.

The house was silent and looked abandoned, and for a moment Amir worried that they might have gotten here too late, but then shouting sounded from inside even before Wolf's men reached the entrances. Then the cops were breaking down the door, pouring in.

To hell with a full minute. Amir stood, ready to charge, just as the black van exploded through the closed garage door, dragging some of the paneling with it. His gun was raised before he realized who was behind the steering wheel.

"It's all right. It's her. It's Isabelle!" he shouted to some of the cops who came rushing back out, and they went back in where gunfire and shouts indicated full-out battle.

The van was next to him, slowing.

He tore the passenger door open and jumped in, not caring one bit if he tore out a couple of stitches. "Keep going!"

She stepped on the gas like she meant it, the tires kicking up gravel behind them, the garage door paneling coming loose as they shot forward.

"Are you hurt?" He was inspecting every inch of her, worried even if there was no visible injury.

"Fine. Where to?" Her hands were shaking. She winced. "I'm not cut out for this. I'm a surgeon, for heaven's sake. My hands *never* shake."

"To the end of the street. I don't want to switch seats here. Too many bullets flying." He glanced back. The old him would have never left a fight in progress. The new him...

She was safe. He was content to let the police handle the rest. All right, not content, but willing. He would have liked nothing more than to stand face-to-face with his enemies and teach them a couple of important lessons about messing with him and the people he cared for.

Bloodlust rose in him.

But he cared more about Isabelle than he cared about revenge. His need to see her safe was stronger than his warrior ancestors' blood, which sang in his veins.

Yes, he cared that much about her. And not just as the mother of his son. Feelings he wasn't familiar with had taken up residence inside his chest, feelings that squeezed his heart with worry when they were apart and filled him with joy at the sight of her. Feelings that, he suspected, were going to complicate everything.

She drove to the corner, then pulled over, laid her arms on the steering wheel and her head over them. Her face was a shade paler than usual. "That was…close. Just give me a second."

"Did anyone hurt you?" He put his gun on the dashboard so he could pull her over and into his arms. They could afford a brief pause. Wolf had brought enough men to take care of whomever had kidnapped Isabelle.

She came willingly to his side, sliding over on the bench seat. "They only took me because they thought you might come for me."

"Of course I would. I know you think that counting on a man is a bad thing. But I am an honorable man. You can count on me."

He would take her back to the resort, to safety,

then go down to the police station and watch as Wolf brought the bastards in, pull whatever strings he could to make sure they stayed incarcerated permanently. He would know who was behind this by the end of today, a thought he found immensely cheering. "Did you recognize any of them?"

"They are the same people who came to the cabin."

"Hired men. Did you overhear anything?"

"They didn't talk much in front of me. I was locked up in the basement alone."

The need to interrogate and punish those men was overwhelming. For the sake of international relations, however, he would leave them to Wolf. But the man who was behind these thugs would answer to him personally; he would see to that. He had every confidence that his friends were on the same page and would put their influence behind him.

The thought that Isabelle could have gotten hurt was unbearable.

"How did you even find me?" she asked. "I didn't think you would. I had the key to the car."

She didn't have those keys now, or her purse, he noticed. "Just as well. They probably put a tracker on the car after we left it in that alley. They couldn't have tracked us to the hospital otherwise. I found you with some help from my friends. I had the van's license-plate number."

"Are your friends back there, in that fight?" A fresh load of worry filled her voice.

"Back at the resort. I'm here with the sheriff's department." She felt wonderful in his arms, like she belonged there. And she did. He would do whatever it took to make her see it.

She lifted her head to look at him. "You decided to trust the police? Doesn't that risk your life and the lives of the other royals? I thought nobody was to be trusted."

"A risk we had to take." He had found that he was willing to risk just about everything for Isabelle.

"But you're all sheiks and princes. I'm just a plain everyday person. I'm not worth all that."

He held her gaze. He couldn't understand why nobody had told her yet how far she was from plain. "You are worth everything to me." The staggering truth of that simple statement caught him off guard.

"Don't look at me like that."

"Like what?"

"Like you want to wrap me in cotton. I was kidnapped and I got away. I did it." She bit her bottom lip, making him want to kiss the spot. "Okay, fine, I do admit wishing that you were there with me. I do understand the importance of teamwork. I rely on it in the O.R. to keep patients alive. You and I together managed to keep ourselves alive in the past two days. I can't argue that we don't make a decent team."

That last sentence pleased him inordinately. He might have even grinned. "You're getting used to me. You'll barely notice that we're married."

She arched one dark, feminine eyebrow. "Somehow I doubt that very sincerely."

"How about we try and see?"

Before she could shoot his proposal down once again, the small window separating the cab from the rest of the van opened and a gun emerged, the barrel pressing against her head.

"Throw the gun out the window," a disembodied voice said from the darkness.

Amir's body clenched. This was not how it was going to end. He silently swore to that.

The blood ran out of Isabelle's face, leaving her skin so light, it was practically translucent. Her blue eyes were wide, her gaze hanging on his face.

His first instinct, as always, was to fight. But Isabelle and her son were too important to him to put at risk. "Everything is going to be fine," he told her. "We are going to do whatever he says."

He took his gun with his right hand, rolled the window down and tossed the weapon out. And while the man's attention was on that, with his left hand Amir surreptitiously pocketed a cell phone that someone had left in the cup holder.

A police car flew by them, sirens blaring, heading toward the house. It was gone way too fast for either of them to catch the driver's attention.

"Pull slowly away from the curb and drive," the man behind the partition told Isabelle. "And don't do anything stupid."

Chapter Eight

She'd been so close to making it. Fear mixed with frustration inside Isabelle as she drove. She'd made it out of the house unseen. She'd gotten the van. Amir was with her. But they were in even more trouble than ever before. She wasn't sure there was an out this time, any way to escape.

"How badly were you shot?" she asked Amir under her breath, noting the bulging bandages under his shirt.

"It's nothing."

"Shut up," the man in the back yelled, then instructed her to take the first road out of town, and from there an insignificant country road she was barely familiar with.

They even left that after a couple of miles, moving on to dirt roads Isabelle had never seen and that led deep into the woods, probably used only by trappers and hunters. Some Texicano family had moved up from the Austin area and had a farm out this way, on the other side of the woods, she thought, but wasn't sure.

They were in the middle of nowhere with an armed kidnapper, in a van that smelled like stale beer and cigarette smoke. He had to have been in the back all along. In the excitement of the moment, she had never thought to check. This was so not her world. She didn't think like some action movie superspy heroine or a Special Forces soldier. She was a soon-to-be mom, bloated and tired, with swollen ankles.

"I demand that you let her go," Amir said in a tone that would make most men want to automatically obey.

It even made Isabelle snap to.

"I demand that you shut up." The jerk in the back sneered at him, obviously not affected. He held the only weapon. He had every reason to be cocky.

"She has nothing to do with this. You don't need her for anything."

Amir was right about that. They'd kidnapped her in that parking garage in the first place only to draw him out, and now they had him. They wanted him dead. They wouldn't have blown up his limousine a month ago if they didn't. And now they wanted her dead, too. She was an asset that had outlived its usefulness, a cumbersome witness. She had no illusions about what would happen next, why they were being taken to an abandoned area. If they survived the next couple of hours, it would be a miracle.

"Faster," the man barked at her.

Fingers in a death grip around the steering wheel, she pushed harder on the gas pedal, but then eased off again little by little, playing for time. "The road is too rough. If I go any faster, I'll bust a tire and then we'll be stuck out here."

She needed to be ready to grab the slightest opportunity, so she kept her eyes on their surroundings, hoping that they would run into someone, the bird-watcher club, those Texicano farmers, anyone she could use as a distraction, anyone who might help.

Unfortunately, no such opportunity presented itself. Not many people ever came out this way, the road little more than a trail.

Then they came around a bend and she spotted a wooden shack up ahead. The worn wood-plank walls and moss-covered roof completely blended into their surroundings. Looked like the structure had been standing here for decades, overgrown with vines and weeds, forlorn in a spooky kind of way.

All she could think of was, *Unabomber's cabin.*

"Stop," the man in the back ordered. "You get out," he told Amir. "One wrong move, you cameljockey terrorist bastard, and I shoot her. You wanna make my day, huh? You wanna make my day?"

"I will do whatever you say." Amir was the picture of calm, opening the door slowly and leaving it open behind him.

"Inside. Now," their captor shouted at him.

Amir did as he was told, disappearing from sight into the darkness of the shack.

Blood thrummed loudly in Isabelle's ears. Why were they being separated?

Keep calm. It's not over yet. Stress and elevated blood pressure were a danger to the baby. She focused on staying composed. She couldn't afford to let the fear rule her. She put a shaky hand on her belly. *Mommy is going to handle this. We're going to be fine.*

"Don't you move." The man kept his gun on her. "I'm getting out the back and comin' around. Don't even think about runnin'."

She wasn't. She could never outrun him on the uneven ground, not nine-months pregnant. But even if she could outrun *him,* she couldn't outrun a bullet.

She used the time while he went around to search the glove compartment, hoping for a weapon of her own. All she found was a Phillips-head screwdriver. Better than nothing. She hid it under her dress just as the man appeared outside her door.

"Get out," he ordered, revealing stained teeth. His lower lip stuck out from the wad of tobacco he was chewing.

He brushed his thinning, greasy hair back with his free hand in a nervous gesture, his red-rimmed eyes darting around. He was nearly as tall as Amir, but Amir was a lot less gaunt, even with his recent illness. This guy had the look of a man who got most of his daily caloric intake in the form of alcoholic beverages. *Completely unstable,* was her thought, not exactly reassuring.

She slipped from the car, keeping an eye on him, holding one hand on her belly, surreptitiously clasping the screwdriver in place under her shirt.

"Get inside. Now!"

A fallen branch or a good-size stone in her path to hit him over the head with would come in handy. She could see neither within reach. Of course, whether she could bend over in a hurry was questionable. She waddled to the shack, eager to be with Amir. His presence had become a comfort to her. Was that wrong? Did it mean that she was slipping into the dreaded dependency trap?

No, she decided. These were extraordinary circumstances. The regular rules of conduct could take a break when you were in the middle of the woods, have been kidnapped and were about ready to have a baby.

She stepped into the semidarkness of the shack, was shoved forward impatiently past Amir, who'd been standing by the door. Before she could take a good look around, the door slammed shut with force. The padlock clicked with a grim finality.

A shiver of foreboding ran down her spine. "Oh, God."

Then Amir was by her side, pulling her into his arms before she could stumble over something. She melted into the familiar scent and shape of him, and remained in his arms, breathing him in, leaning against his strength. They were still alive and the baby was unharmed. For now that was all that mattered.

She waited for her eyes to adjust to the darkness, trying to come up with a plan and failing.

"I got him," the man said outside their locked room.

So he wasn't alone. Someone must have been here, hiding, waiting for them. Escape just got another notch more difficult.

The man kept on talking, swearing deliberately. Nobody ever answered.

"He's talking on the phone," Amir whispered next to her ear.

She sagged against him in relief as she listened, hoping for a clue, something they could use to get away from this place.

"Damn police raided the house. The pregnant bitch snatched the van. I was sleepin' in the back, mindin' my own business. With everyone yappin' in the house, too damned loud to get any shut-eye in there."

A moment of silence.

"That's what I'm sayin'. I hear someone get in, and next thing I know, the witch is goin' through the garage door. Then the sheik bastard jumps in. I recognized him from the picture you been showin'."

Another moment of silence.

"Out at the old McClusky shed. Can I kill 'em yet? No sense in waitin'. Hotter than a whorehouse on nickel night out here." He waited for the answer.

Amir pushed her behind him with a gentleness that touched her, standing between her and the door, ready to face imminent attack. Ready to take a bullet for her. Her heart turned over in her chest. She pulled out the screwdriver and gripped it in her hand, prepared to help him fight whatever would come next.

"Don't worry," the man was saying outside, his tone betraying that he was disappointed with the response he'd gotten. "They ain't goin' anywhere. They'll wait."

Then there was nothing but silence.

She swallowed hard, lowering the screwdriver as her heartbeat slowed. They'd been granted a reprieve.

She stepped away from Amir, and after a minute or two, when her eyes adjusted to the minimal light, she looked around her new prison. The place was worse than the basement office, dirtier and full of spiders. A nasty, dusty camp bed took up the far wall, the only place to sit. A rusty woodstove hid in the corner. Cigarette butts and candy wrappers littered the floor, along with other indistinguishable old garbage.

She so didn't want to die in a place like this. She wanted her baby to be born, for them to have a future. She wrapped her arms around her belly and blinked back her tears.

AMIR PULLED OUT THE phone he'd lifted from the van earlier and dialed. He asked for Prince Efraim's suite in a whisper when the other end was picked up.

"Where the hell are you?" Darek asked.

"We're out in the woods, at the end of some country road. At the McClusky shed. Jake Wolf should know where it is. If you can't reach Wolf, get a GPS on this phone signal."

He wanted to say a lot more, but he didn't want

the kidnapper to hear him, figure out he had the phone. That phone was their lifeline for the time being.

"I'll tell the others. They just went down to the conference room. Stefan called a meeting with the security we still trust and the police. I was about to head down there myself."

"Hurry. Only one armed guard here now, but reinforcements are coming." Frustration was eating him from the inside out.

Were he alone, he would kick the door open and rip the bastard's head off. But he needed to stay calm so Isabelle wouldn't be injured in any fight. A stray bullet could easily find her. So he gritted his teeth and resolved to bide his time, no matter how much he hated hiding in the shed.

"Thank God you grabbed that phone," Isabelle said as he hung up. "Who did you reach?"

"Prince Darek." He shoved the phone into his pocket, then moved to the wall and began systematically searching every square inch of wall and floor. Just because he couldn't fight, it didn't mean he was cursed with complete inactivity.

"One of the princes for the summit?"

"Another friend. We all grew up together, actually." Then Darek's father went mad with greed. His country, Saruk, was the largest in the region. A few years back King Kalil had decided it would be a good idea to annex the smaller island nations to gain more power for himself. Darek wasn't like him, but all that tension had soured their friendship.

Until recently. It seemed they could still count on him when they were in trouble.

"I thought the news said only five princes came."

"He only arrived recently." And probably in secret. "He heard about all the difficulties and flew over to help. True friendship is proven when one is in trouble," he said, quoting an old Jamalan proverb, as he squatted to look under the bed, feeling guilty that he had, on occasion, doubted Darek's sincerity. But the man did stand up to the test. He was here, ready to do whatever was needed.

"You don't know how I envy you." The words flew from Isabelle's lips on a sigh.

He looked up. "For my friends?" Was she lonely? At that masquerade at the resort where they'd met, she'd been surrounded by a group of friends. For the first time, it occurred to him that she might have missed those friends while she'd been taking care of him at her father's cabin. He would make sure they had an open invitation to visit his palace whenever they pleased. He wanted Isabelle happy.

"I envy your ability to squat. Or move freely in general," she said in a wry tone. "These days, I'm happy if I can bend over to fasten my sandals in the morning. What are you doing down there?"

"Looking for a way out, and for any tool that could help." Plan B. They were running out of time. He needed to be ready for whatever might happen next, especially if something happened before Darek and the others arrived.

THEY WERE FINE. They had made contact. Help was on the way.

Isabelle held out the screwdriver. Amir must not have seen it in the dark. "How is this for a tool?"

He grinned as he came over. "Amazing." He put his hands over hers but didn't take the tool. Instead, he pulled her to him and kissed her.

His lips were firm and warm on hers, knowing. He was an excellent kisser. She certainly hadn't forgotten that. And he seemed even better now than she remembered. Her pulse raced. Her mind turned to mush in less than two seconds. She placed her hands on his chest, and he must have correctly read that as a sign of surrender, because he deepened the kiss.

Her whole body tingled. She had dreamed of him often in the past nine months, but this was so much better than any of her dreams. He was real, his chest solid under her fingertips, his heart beating fast against her palm.

She wanted him. Nine-months pregnant and she wanted him so much she moaned his name. She probably should have been ashamed of herself, but she couldn't manage an emotion as complicated as that at the moment. Primal need ruled her. Yes, she wanted him. This was what she wanted.

But how long could this tumult of emotions and need last? her last sober brain cell asked. She didn't want to fall into some fantasy of the two of them together forever, unreasonably happy and all that.

Things like that weren't real. Trouble was, she could see it. She really could.

"I don't want to fall in love with you," she whispered against his lips without meaning to, the words bubbling up from her subconscious. And scaring her. She pulled away.

He watched her from under hooded eyelids, desire etched clearly on his face. She would be a goner if he kept looking at her like that. She turned from him in an attempt to hang on to the last remnants of her sanity.

"It would be too easy to fall for the whole 'protected by the powerful sheik' thing," she said quickly. "Who doesn't want that? But then, eventually... And life isn't meant to be a search for safe, anyway. You have to face the challenges and grow." Exactly why she'd gone to medical school and become a doctor instead of marrying one, like her mother.

Even if all she'd wanted to be was Annie Oakley. Well, when she'd been really young. In elementary and middle school, being a famous female sharpshooter or a cowgirl had been her career dreams. Then the more she understood all that her father did for others, the more she wanted to be like him. Never like her mother. She even made a point to do poorly in gym class. She didn't want any talk that she would be an athlete and follow in her mother's footprints.

She turned back to him slowly and watched as his eyes narrowed.

"Let me understand this. You fear that marrying me might make you too safe?"

She didn't *exactly* mean that, but close enough. She nodded.

"I do wish for your safety." His tone was somber. "But I fear I have failed at every attempt to keep you out of trouble. Look at the danger I consistently put you in. Look at where we are even at this moment."

"You didn't put me in danger."

He shook his head with impatience. "You're in danger because of me. You are here because I came back to you, because you saved my life and sheltered me." He looked pained.

"No matter what happens, I'm not going to regret that."

For a second, she thought he would take her into his arms again. But instead he stepped away from her and continued the thorough search of the shed. "I'm going to get us out of here."

She rubbed against the pain in her lower back, then sat on the dubious-looking bed. Getting on her hands and knees to help Amir search the floor was out of the question. She had to let him take care of that. Not that she expected him to find much, anyway. The shed was pretty bare.

He ran his hand over the same spot he'd just searched a second ago, then went still.

"What is it?"

He yanked a dusty rug aside and felt the floorboards with his hands. "I think there's a secret door here," he whispered.

He used the screwdriver for leverage but didn't succeed at first.

"Is there anything I can do to help?"

"Rest."

"I'm not completely useless, you know."

"I never said that." He tried another angle, wedging the screwdriver into some invisible gap, then using the side of his fist as a hammer to drive it in a little.

Then she heard a small pop and the wood creaked. Too loudly? She held her breath. Nobody came from outside. No indication that the man out there had heard them. Amir leaned onto the screwdriver's handle. And after another small pop, the panel of wood flooring did come up, leaving a two-foot-by-three-foot gap in front of him that she could barely make out in the darkness.

She leaned forward, excitement coursing through her veins. "What's down there?"

"I can't see, but the space is pretty big."

Some old conversations she'd had with her father came back suddenly. "You know, old McClusky was rumored to be a moonshiner back in the day."

Amir glanced up with a questioning look.

"Alcohol was illegal for more than a decade in the U.S. Didn't last long, but while it did, a lot of people made money distilling their own booze in out-of-the-way shacks like this. Some still do, just for the hell of it."

He stepped over the hole and lowered himself carefully. "Islam does not allow alcohol at all. We believe it ruins too many good men. Too many families."

She couldn't argue with that, knowing well what alcohol and drugs had done to her mother. She'd been thinking more and more about her lately. Probably because she was about to become a mother herself. But now wasn't a time for dwelling on the past. She needed to put those old regrets away.

"Look out for snakes," she suggested. As many spiders as there were up here, she couldn't imagine what all might live down there. She wouldn't go down for anything, which wasn't an issue, since her belly wouldn't fit through the opening, anyway. She could take blood and gore, but she usually screamed her head off when she was faced with a centipede.

"Looks like a whole other room." Things rattled down there in the dark.

"Does it have an outside exit?"

"I see a section that's walled up. Maybe it used to lead to a tunnel."

Her back was screaming bloody murder. She lay down on the bed gingerly. It held. She closed her eyes, exhausted. Of course, she was always tired these days. Growing a baby inside her was hard work, taxing her body.

The soft noises Amir made below comforted her. She wasn't alone in this. She relaxed a little. Then she relaxed all the way.

Chapter Nine

Bare and breezy wasn't exactly her style. She so regretted giving in to Janie about the costumes. She normally strove for a conservative and professional look at the hospital. Isabelle tugged a few strategically placed veils into place and looked around the charity ball, reminding herself that they were doing this for the right reason. The pediatric wing needed new equipment. She was happy to be part of this.

Then the short hairs at her nape rose and she turned, feeling someone's attention on her as surely as if he'd called her name. Her eyes found him immediately. His dark gaze burned into hers from across the room. Air caught in her lungs. She couldn't look away.

He was tall, his dark hair matching his eyes, olive complexion, regal bearing. He was dressed in a flowing white caftan thickly embroidered with gold. He looked like some sort of a Middle Eastern prince. That their costumes matched didn't escape her. Around her, the other girls from general surgery twittered, having obviously spotted him.

"Who is *that?*" Abby asked.

"Mine." Lynn pushed forward as the man started for them.

But he held Isabelle's gaze, not sparing a single glance at the others.

He held out his long-fingered hand for her, and mesmerized, she put her hand in his.

"It's hot in here. Shall we take a turn out on the balcony?" His voice had a slight exotic accent, deeply rich and melodic.

She simply nodded. There did seem to be a sudden lack of air in the room, she noticed.

"You work in the hospital?" he asked once they were outside. He didn't release her.

"Yes." The cool night air felt good. "You?" Although, if she'd seen him here before, no way would she have forgotten it.

"I'm from Jamala. I'm only visiting. Are you a doctor?"

"Yes." Way to go with the one-word sentences.

"That is still rare in my country. Women in medical school, I mean." He gave a smile that went straight to her knees.

They talked about the hospital, then health care in his own country. He was informed, intelligent, articulate. And she found that they agreed on a great many things. Although he set her nerve endings buzzing, talking with him was incredibly comfortable.

He took her empty champagne glass and set it on

one of the stone balustrades. "I have better champagne in my suite. Will you join me?"

She knew what he was asking.

She nodded, half numb, and didn't know where she got the temerity. Maybe they would just talk.

"Good." There came that smile again as he drew her behind him. "I want to kiss you in private."

Heat spread through her. She seemed helpless under whatever spell he had woven over her.

They took the elevator upstairs but they weren't alone. She pulled her hand from his, not wanting others to see and set hospital tongues wagging. He seemed to understand and waited patiently until the others left. Then he took her hand again and kissed it.

Her pulse jumped at the contact, at the warmth of his lips.

Soon they were off the elevator and in his suite, and apparently it was time for that kiss, because he didn't waste any time bending his head to meet her lips.

Oh, sweet heaven.

He wasn't the first man to have kissed her, but no kiss she'd ever received had been like this. She felt like she had just stepped, eyes wide, into a hurricane. Every bit of shyness, resistance and common sense was instantly blown away.

Need like that shouldn't exist, she thought, dazed. And more than a little scared. He was infinitely more than she had expected. He explored her and claimed her as his own sovereign territory. He ruled her senses. Her lungs were fighting for air by the time he pulled away.

"It's… I'm normally not like this," she said, bewildered, not knowing what to do next. Her knees were too shaky to stand, but she couldn't make herself head straight for the sprawling couch, and she barely even dared looking at the immense bed through the open bedroom door. "I've never followed a stranger to his room before," she admitted.

"Nothing will happen that you do not wish," he assured her immediately, but his eyes were ablaze with desire.

Nothing that she didn't wish. Trouble was, she wished…*everything*.

Which was so completely irresponsible.

He walked to the bar and poured them champagne, a much better brand than downstairs in the ballroom, as he had promised. The bubbles seemed to go straight to her head. As if her head wasn't swimming already.

All her life she had held back, stuck to the rules and then some, always done the right thing. Now she sipped the bubbly, preparing to do something so completely out of character, she could scarcely believe it. He was at the stereo system, turning on some sultry, sweet music that snuck right under her skin. She finished the delicious champagne.

When he came back to her, he held out a hand. "Dance with me."

Okay, she could do dancing. Dancing was fine. They would dance, talk a little more, and then she was out of here. She set down her glass and let him pull her close.

Their bodies touching full length, for the first time, was a shock, a quickly spreading fire. But she didn't pull away. He smelled like the sea. The alcohol truly must have gone to her head, she thought. They were in the middle of Wyoming.

His gaze caressed every inch of her face as they swayed to the music. "I feel as if I have known you for a hundred years."

She tried to laugh that off, point out that it wasn't a terribly original pickup line as far as those went, but couldn't. Because she felt the same.

She felt as if she'd just come home, into safe port, after having been lost on some vast, inhospitable ocean. She shook her head slightly. That had to be just the champagne talking.

"So you save people all day?" His voice was rich and seductive. "Who saves you?"

That prickled something inside her. "I don't need to be saved."

He gave a low laugh. "Everybody needs to be saved a little."

Was he talking about himself? A tragic past maybe? She forgot to ask when he kissed her again.

This could not be real. In real life there were no men like him, no kisses like this. If there were, she would have heard about it. All her previous encounters with men seemed so pitiful in comparison that they didn't even bear thinking about. There were no other men. Only him.

He tasted her lips over and over again, conquered her mouth without effort, sent her senses spiraling out of control, needing what his kiss promised. Needing it so much it scared her.

She pulled away. Drew a quick breath and searched his gaze for a clue as to what he was thinking. Saw nothing but heat.

"Too fast?"

She nodded. *And not fast enough.*

"How about if we just stick to dancing?"

She agreed to that. Already she missed his arms around her. But not for long. They enfolded her quickly enough, as if he'd missed her, too.

"Much better," he whispered in her ear, his warm breath ruffling a few stray strands of hair at her nape, sending tingles down her spine.

"I'm not sure what's happening," she whispered back.

"Mercury in retrograde?"

"What?" She was clueless about astrology.

"Pay no mind to me. I have no idea what it means. I have a sister who sometimes talks about that sort of thing."

The song ended; another began. Neither gave a thought to stopping. They danced through that song, then the next and the next. She had no idea what he was thinking. She was thinking that she could get used to this.

"Would it be all right if I kissed you again?" he asked after a while.

That seemed like the exact perfect thing. She tilted her head up to him.

This time the flood of sensations didn't scare her as much as the first time. She hung on to him and rode the wave.

His lips kissed a trail to her ear, nibbled her sensitive earlobe. Shivers of desire ran down the length of her body as his hot mouth moved down her neck, inch by inch, with care.

"I could kiss your neck all day," he murmured.

She seriously doubted she could take it all day. Her knees were already buckling. And that was before his long, knowing fingers slowly danced up her rib cage. As flimsy as her costume was, not much separated skin from skin.

Then his hand found the gap between the layers of veils and his heated palm branded her. She opened her eyes, startled, only to realize that he had danced them into the bedroom, where the most amazingly large bed she'd ever seen waited.

"What do you wish?" His voice was a rasp, an urgent whisper that tickled along her nerve endings.

She reached up to his white caftan and parted it bravely.

Hunger burned in his gaze. "Anytime you wish to stop, we will."

She believed him. She felt 100 percent safe with him, which was sheer insanity, given the brevity of their acquaintance. But she saw dozens of patients every day and considered herself a fair judge of character. She trusted her instincts.

She pushed the caftan off his shoulders, watched the lustrous material pool at their feet, then placed her palms against his chest, on the light linen shirt he was wearing. She could feel his heartbeat. Slow and steady.

"Come," he said, and she melted into his embrace.

He removed her veils one by one, expertly, as if unwrapping a gift. "Exquisite."

She had nothing left but a sequined bra with matching panties. She pressed against him so he couldn't take a good look at her.

He gently pushed her away with a low chuckle. "That's not going to work. I want to see—" his gaze darkened "—everything."

And as he stood before her, tall and heart-achingly handsome, she couldn't say she didn't want to see the same. She snuck her hands under his shirt, her palms gliding up the smooth pane of his abdomen, over ripples of muscles. Her fingertips tingled.

"More?" he asked when she hesitated.

She covered his masculine chest willingly.

Whatever he did for a living, he didn't do a lot of sitting around behind a desk at the office. He had the body of a man who was physically active. He had a body that could make most women weep, honestly.

And he was here, with her.

"Why me?" Her insecurities pushed the words to her lips.

"Was there anyone else in the room?" he asked lightly.

She felt the same. Once she'd spotted him, it had been as if the rest of the room had disappeared.

His hands caressed her shoulders and moved down her back, to the clasp of her bra. "May I?"

She grew uncertain again. "Wait." She already felt way underdressed compared to him.

He must have guessed her thoughts, because he reached for the bottom of his shirt and pulled it over his head, tossed it to the floor. "Better?"

Oh, was it ever. Her gaze got lost on the panes of his chest for a long minute.

A pleased smile played on his lips. He waited. He didn't push her, not with a look, not with a gesture.

She turned her back to him, pulling her hair aside, offering him the clasp. "Please."

He ran his fingers around the outline of the material first, teasing her, tormenting her, setting her skin on fire. Then, at long last, she felt the pressure of the elastic give.

She held the cups in place in front as she turned. "I'm sorry. I'm too…" She wasn't sure what she should say. Inexperienced? Self-conscious?

"You're perfect."

Again, she moved to him, pressed against him to avoid his gaze. He kissed her, kissed a path down her neck, reaching between them and lightly pulling away her bra.

Her breath caught.

Skin to skin.

Heat throbbed low inside her belly.

"I'm going take you to the bed. Tell me if that's too fast."

She didn't say anything.

Slowly he reached under her thighs and lifted her up, wrapped her unsteady legs around his slim waist. His hard length pressed against her aching core, leaving no doubt how much he wanted her. Yet his patience didn't waver for a second.

He settled her in the middle of the bed, then lay next to her, coming up on his elbow, taking in every inch of her. "A work of art. I never understood, until now, why artists say that about the human body."

The compliment was so outrageous, she couldn't respond to it. Her body was far from perfect. After her shift was done, more often than not, she was too tired to exercise. And all too often too tired to make and eat something healthy instead of a microwave dinner.

He placed a hand on her abdomen, and her skin immediately heated; need tugged at her. He drew slow circles, up and up, until he reached her breast. He outlined one first, then the other. Then he drew concentric circles with his index finger until he reached her nipple.

She arched into his hand until his palm covered her breast completely. Almost more than she could bear. And then he dipped his head with a wicked smile and tasted the other nipple.

A low moan tore deep from her throat.

Insanity. What she was doing here was pure

madness. And she wanted more of it. She wasn't sure why now, why with this man, but she did know that he was different from all the others she'd met.

His lips tugged and suckled; his fingers rubbed and teased. She buried her hands in his thick black hair, luxuriating in the silky strands.

Then his hands moved and his fingers were on her panties, tugging them down. Only then did she realize that his pants and underwear were already gone. When did that happen?

His body was pure perfection, tan skin stretching over lean muscles.

He kissed her one more time, deeply, until her head was spinning and red-hot need throbbed in every cell. Was she really going to do this? Did she have the strength and the will to stop? No, she didn't. This was what she wanted.

He pulled away, only to kneel between her legs. One hand under each thigh, he bent her knees. Out of nowhere, a foil wrapper materialized in his hand.

"Are you sure?" His dark eyes were hooded; his voice was a thick whisper that held all kinds of promises, his amazing body was hard and more than ready.

Glorious was the first word that came to mind. "I'm sure."

Chapter Ten

Isabelle woke with a start. Her cheeks felt hot; her thoughts were jumbled. A long second passed before she fully transitioned from her erotic dream to stark reality.

Amir was coming up from the dugout under the shack. "I found a couple of these." He had brought an empty bottle with him. "Are you well?" He stopped as he took her in. "Does anything hurt?"

"Fell asleep for a minute."

"I thought so. You were mumbling."

Her heart nearly stopped. "Anything interesting?" she asked nonchalantly.

"If it was, it was in another language." He grinned. "What do you think of this?"

She eyed the bottle doubtfully at first, then realized it could come in handy for hitting someone over the head. This had obviously been Amir's intention, since he was testing the balance of the bottle in his hand now, holding it like a baseball bat.

She was a doctor. Her first thought was to heal and not to harm. She held a hand out now as she

stood. "You keep the screwdriver. I'll take that."
And stop thinking about that dream. Now. Pronto.
Immediately. Their current situation needed her full
attention. "So a screwdriver and a bottle."

Amir's friends were on the way. If the guy outside had any nasty ideas before help came, at last
they had a way now to defend themselves. With
both of them armed and the element of surprise
on their side, who knew what could happen? They
might even make it.

Amir strode to the window and peered through
the gap the nasty blanket didn't cover. Then he
moved to the bed and grabbed the mattress, laid it
against the front wall of the shed. "When the rescue
team gets here, we need to take cover. There'll be
too many bullets flying out there." He grinned suddenly. "Sorry. I know you don't want to be protected. I don't think I can stop trying. It is not a bad
thing."

She took a couple of slow breaths and made a
concentrated effort to clear the last remnants of her
dream from her brain. *Okay. Gone.*

"It's fine. It's teamwork. I get it." She wished
there was more light to see the smile that bloomed
on his face.

"You know what else is all about teamwork?
Marriage." His smile transformed into a wicked
grin.

"Quit while you're ahead," she warned him. The
rest of a smart-alecky response was on the tip of

her tongue, but a cramp started low in her belly just then, distracting her.

She put her hand on the spot and tried to massage the cramp away.

"What is it?" Amir was by her side in a split second, placing his hands on hers. He had strong hands with long, aristocratic fingers. Exactly as she remembered in her dream.

She could see those hands wrapped around the steering wheel of some superexpensive sports car, or reining in a wild camel. Or holding their baby. An emotion she didn't want to acknowledge welled up inside her chest. She looked away from their joined hands. "More Braxton Hicks."

"I don't like these practice contractions. If they make you wince, then what about the real thing? I don't want you to be in pain."

"I'll deal with it." She fully planned on getting an epidural. She was a doctor, very comfortable around drugs. In all the years she'd worked at the hospital, she hadn't heard of a single adverse reaction to the new family of painkillers they now used during childbirth.

"It would be better if my heir was born in Jamala. But either way, I'll be there to hold your hand."

She looked up, surprised. "No, you won't." That wasn't at all how she had planned it.

His face turned stony. "He is my son."

"But you're hardly my soul mate and best friend. We barely know each other. Giving birth is a personal, intimate thing."

His facial muscles tightened even more. "I'm the father."

She pulled away from him. "I can't relax around you, okay?"

He blinked as he watched her. "I make you nervous? But all I want is whatever is best for you."

Not exactly nervous, but out of sorts, unsure of herself, sometimes dazed, sometimes tingly. She didn't like it.

"I will see my son born. A husband's place is at his wife's side at such a time."

"We're not getting married."

"The right thing…" He paused, probably remembering that this was the argument that hadn't gotten him anywhere so far. He drew a slow breath and changed tactics. "You cannot tell me that when I kiss you—"

"Stop." Okay. He had something there. Possibly the root of their communication problem. She kept letting him kiss her. How could he understand that she meant business when she said no, if she kept giving in to his amazing kisses? "We're not kissing anymore," she informed him, not without regret.

"The hell we aren't." He backed her right up against the wall.

He braced his hands on each side of her, lowering his head slowly, holding her gaze. A slow thrumming started in her blood. But when his lips were an inch from hers, he stopped. His warm breath fanned her face, his nearness wreaking havoc on her senses. Heat burned in his eyes, emanated from his powerful body.

She didn't want to want him, but she did.

He, on the other hand, didn't bother to hide his desire for her, at all.

"We *will* be together," he told her with a voice of smooth, hot velvet.

Knees, don't fail me now. She drew a slow, shallow breath. His lips were so distractingly close. She felt her eyelids drift closed of their own volition. *No. Not going to happen.* But she couldn't have moved to save her life as his mouth came closer and closer to hers.

A soft brush of his lips was all she got, which left her ravenously hungry.

But he was already pulling away. "This is neither the time nor the place."

Now he is going to start sounding reasonable?

She could have cried with frustration, but before she could as much as yell at him for putting her in this state, the sound of an arriving car interrupted them. They went to the window together.

A black SUV rolled into view, men jumping out even before the engine was cut.

"Darek. We'll be fine now," Amir said next to her, relief in his voice. "I don't see the others, but they must be around, out of sight. It's about to begin. Get down behind the mattress."

But the new arrivals didn't look like they were preparing for a fight. In fact, the man who had brought them here walked right up to Darek. They looked pretty friendly.

Amir muttered a couple of heated words in his own language.

"What happened?" She turned to him, bewildered.

His face might as well have been carved of stone. "We've been betrayed."

And as he turned, she saw a dark spot on his shoulder, reached out a hand and found some wetness. "What's this?"

"The bullet hole. It's not that bad."

He must have aggravated the wound while exploring the hidden room below the shack. "You can't lose blood. Stop moving. Lie down on the bed."

He shook his head. "If things don't go well in the next five minutes, I'm not going to live long enough to bleed out," he said, as if that was supposed to relax her.

Amir stepped in front of Isabelle to protect her as much as possible. He tucked the screwdriver into his waistband at his back. "Don't let them see that bottle."

"Why?" She sounded ready to fight.

His mind was still trying to catch up with the fact that Darek was the enemy. Darek wouldn't have told Stephan and the others about the phone call. His true friends still had no idea where he was.

"Don't want to force their hand when we're at a disadvantage. We are outnumbered and they're better armed. If we can hold on until darkness, our chances of breaking out will be much better. At least some of them might be sleeping. And they won't be able to see as well."

"Plus you might break through to the tunnel by then," she added and shoved the bottle under her armpit under the shirt, holding it there with her arm, out of sight, but close enough to grab if a fight was forced on them.

He turned to the door, standing with legs slightly apart, square in the middle of the room, keeping his face impassive as the door opened. *Keep calm. Control the situation.*

But the blood boiled in his veins. He couldn't help one small comment as Darek appeared. "I should have known. As they say, the apple doesn't fall far from the tree."

"So it doesn't," the black-hearted prince of Saruk agreed easily, not appearing to be struggling with a crisis of conscience.

"You'd betray your friends?"

"Friends are friends, but I'll always do what's best for my own people. You'd do the same." As usual, he was dressed like a movie star, a superior grin on his face. "History remembers winners. It doesn't care by what method they win."

He brushed lint off his double-breasted suit jacket, able to notice a small detail like that at a moment like this. He always placed great importance on his appearance. He was known to fly in a full new wardrobe from London several times a year, through good times and bad, even in times of famine.

Not that his country had seen famine for some time now. In fact, they had been doing rather well lately.

"Saruk is a big country. You already have everything you need." Amir watched the man's eyes instead of the weapon in his hands. He'd been in enough fights in his younger years to know that it was the eyes where everything was decided.

"Big country, big headache. More administrative costs, more everything." Darek shrugged.

And Amir realized that he had probably been planning the attack for a while now, had had plenty of time to justify it in his twisted brain. It would be a waste of time to try to appeal to his conscience. He was like his father, after all, and didn't have any.

"We're going to need those underwater oil rights, I'm afraid," the traitor was saying.

Of course. "It's not up to me. Those rights are governed by COIN." He had created the Coalition of Island Nations with his friends for that specific purpose. To manage those oil rights together and to facilitate other economically favorable treaties, including those designed to boost tourism and industry.

Darek raised his gun. "Not to worry. I'm planning on calling a meeting in the morning. Why don't you hand over that phone you called me from? We wouldn't want you to be ruining my big surprise, now, would we?"

Everything in Amir screamed to fight, even if it meant certain death. But he kept coming back to the same thing over and over again. Once he was dead, who would protect Isabelle and his son? Teeth grinding, he tossed the phone to Darek, pushing redial. His last call had been to Efraim's suite. If Efraim picked up, he would hear what was going on here.

But Darek must have caught the small move and turned off the phone, tossed it down and ground it under his heel until the slim unit came apart and lay broken, in pieces. "There comes a time when every man must accept his fate," he lectured in a tone of superiority.

"You're not going to get away with this." He would get the bastard. And if he couldn't because he was dead, his friends would avenge him. Betrayal on this scale would not be forgiven.

But Darek's arrogant smile only widened. "We'll just have to agree to disagree on that, I'm afraid." Then he looked Isabelle over from head to toe, taking his time, openly leering. "Pretty. And resourceful, from what I hear. Then again, you always had good taste in women. She'll be a shame to waste."

His gaze hesitated on Isabelle's breasts, which were swollen with pregnancy. "Still, in this case I don't think her beauty will save her." He sounded almost regretful. "She carries your bastard. I'm afraid, I can't allow that."

He turned back to Amir and continued. "You

must die without an heir, so when I annex Jamala, there will be nothing more natural than for me to become her ruler. I shall save an orphaned nation. A hundred years from now, history books will be calling me the *Savior Prince.*" He gave a dark, nefarious smile that would have fit a silver-screen villain perfectly.

Anger pushed Amir forward a step. But Darek had already moved back and the door slammed closed in his face. The padlock clicked shut. They were trapped again.

He slammed his fist against the rough-hewn wood, ignoring the slivers that dug under his skin, reminding himself that a prince didn't swear in front of a lady under any circumstances.

"I swear to my ancestors that I will see you dead for this," he called through the door.

But Darek was already on the phone, ordering a helicopter to a nearby field for the following morning.

Probably the faster to escape after the bastard killed them.

Isabelle peered into the hidden, nearly pitch-dark space below the floorboards. She could barely make out Amir.

"Why didn't he kill us right here and now?"

"You don't take the bait out of the trap until you've trapped whatever you are hunting. His plan could still go wrong. But as long as he has us, he knows my friends will come to him eventually."

Glass shattered as he broke a bottle against a wall. "I'll see if I can loosen a few rocks. There might be a tunnel behind this wall."

"I wish I could help."

"Rest."

The air coming up from the hole was chilly and musty. She could hear a mouse or some other rodent scurry across the packed-dirt floor down there.

"Is it working?" She tried to see better.

"Not fast enough." He grunted with effort.

"How about the screwdriver?" She bent with effort and extended the tool down into the hole. The tips of her fingers touched Amir's as he reached up. Heat suffused her body. She snatched her hand away. "Do you think this will work?"

He moved back to the wall where he'd been working. "Darek said he's calling a meeting for the morning. We have the rest of the day and all night. There's either a tunnel behind this wall or there isn't. We have to at least try. It's the best chance we have."

"Don't hurt your shoulder."

"Is that doctor's orders?" he teased, injecting a moment of humor into the tense situation.

"Don't make me come down there."

"You can't yet. But we'll widen the opening in the floor if the tunnel down here works out."

Yet another obstacle. But she refused to become discouraged. She wasn't just fighting for herself here. She was fighting for Amir and her baby. "I'll stand by the window and let you know if anyone's coming."

She grabbed the neck of the bottle Amir had given her earlier and felt better for having taken some measure of control back. The next person who came through that door and threatened them was going to regret it.

"Don't push yourself too hard. You don't need to be standing," Amir called up to Isabelle as he wedged the screwdriver under the smallest of the rocks and pressed down hard on the handle. The busted bottle he'd first tried had been little help, but the screwdriver seemed to be doing the trick. The rock moved a little.

"This is going to work," he told her, trying to sound reassuring while knowing there were at least a dozen things that could go wrong, knowing that their chances for failure were a hundred times greater than their chances for escape.

He refused to accept it.

He did make progress, but much slower than he had anticipated. Minutes passed as he worked on the rocks as quietly as he could so the people outside wouldn't suspect anything. "Why don't you try to get some sleep? You will need your strength later."

"I'm too nervous to sleep. I'm a great sleeper usually. I can sleep in the on-call room in between surgeries like nobody's business."

He pressed his lips together. It shouldn't be like this. His future wife should be comfortably resting at the palace, surrounded by help who cared for her and spoiled her. She should most certainly not be in any sort of discomfort or danger.

But the best he could do right now was to take her mind off the men outside the shack.

"When you're not taking care of someone at your father's cabin, where do you live?"

"I have a small condo near the hospital. Actually, it overlooks the ambulance bay. Some of the neighbors complain sometimes, but it doesn't bother me. I can sleep right through ambulance sirens."

"Wish you could sleep now."

"Not even drowsy. I miss my place," she added after a minute. "I haven't had a chance to stop in lately. I'm sure the lemon tree the nurses gave me for my birthday is dead."

"The royal palace of Jamala is surrounded by lemon trees. It's on the highest point of the island. The windows of our private quarters look to the east. French doors lead to a covered terrace." He felt a pang of homesickness just talking about it. "We'll have some of our meals served there. From that spot, you can see forever, the Mediterranean Sea stretching to the horizon. You will like that."

"I might come and see it someday," she allowed.

He grinned in the darkness. "The pink marble bathtub is sunk in the floor and is bigger than this shack." Was that a sigh he heard from up there?

He kept on working, but he kept up with telling her about the country he was willing to die or kill for. "It's a small country. Trade and tourism are big things for us. The people are very friendly, still live at a slower pace than people of the industrialized West. Honor and faith have meaning."

"They have meaning in Wyoming, too."

"I know." He didn't mean to offend her. "I can't help being biased. I love my country." And Darek wasn't going to get it. Not now, not ever. "My son will inherit the throne," he said with force.

"We'll see," was the response from above.

She wasn't exactly jumping up and down with excitement at the prospect, but she wasn't as vehement as before about rejecting everything he had to offer. Maybe they were finally making progress.

"You will like my sister, Saida. She's thoroughly Americanized. I let her attend university here, and now it seems she's engaged to some Wyoming lawman. Jake Wolf. I'm not sure what to think of it," he admitted.

He had always thought Saida would marry a prince, had even hoped it might be one of his friends. But since he was marrying Isabelle, and knew now how important that was to him even if honor and his heir were taken out of the equation, he couldn't exactly tell Saida to marry for the sake of an alliance.

"Let her have her happiness. Jake is a good man. And good-looking," was the answer from above.

"You know him?" Out of the blue, jealousy hit him square in the chest.

"Not well. But I know his reputation. He's an honest man."

Amir relaxed. Then something else occurred to

him. "So you really didn't see anyone else all this time that I was gone?" At the time, those months had seemed short, his schedule filled with back-to-back trips and meetings. But in hindsight, nine months was a very long stretch of time to leave a woman as beautiful as Isabelle.

"Between work and caring for my dying father, I didn't have much energy for dating."

Amazing how good that made him feel, even while regretting all the hardship she had to face. "There can be no other. Ever."

"Right, Mr. Throwback-to-the-Middle-Ages." He could practically see her roll her blue eyes up there. "And how about your harem?"

Did she sound jealous? Another ping of hope came to life inside him. "What about it?"

Her squeak was very unlike the serious-doctor demeanor she usually projected. "You have a harem?"

"Well, technically…" He tried to keep laughter out of his voice.

"You have a harem? I can't believe this! How could you? Are you kidding? Oh, God—"

"If you would let me finish, I could tell you that there's a centuries-old harem attached to the palace that was left behind after the Ottoman invasion. It's currently used as a museum." He paused. "I only want one woman." Her.

No response came to that.

"No one in my family had multiple wives for as far back as I can remember," he said, trying to

reassure her further. He wanted her to be comfortable with him, with his culture. It all might seem
strange to her, but it was his heritage and he was
proud of it. "You'll be my one and only."

Again, she stayed silent.

He didn't like that. At the very least, they needed
to keep the conversation open on the issue. They
had a difference of opinion about their future together, a difference of opinion based on some misunderstandings that they had to work out. They
were two intelligent people; they should be able to
come up with a reasonable solution between them.
All he needed was for her to give their marriage a
chance.

He understood why she might have misgivings,
but he was unwilling to let her slip through his
fingers. Maybe she just needed a reminder. "Last
year, at that masquerade ball, you wanted me."

"Yes," was the small response.

And he appreciated that she was the kind of
woman who wouldn't deny that, wouldn't pretend
that she didn't know what he was talking about.
"Couldn't things be like that between us again?"

"Everything is different now."

"How?"

"You're a sheik. I'm pregnant."

"It's still just you and me. One man and one
woman who are attracted to each other, who are
going to have a child together."

"What you want is… It's not how I planned my

life. My life is at Dumont General. That is my hospital. This is my country. My home is Wyoming."

Sing "The Star-Spangled Banner" and all that, he thought, frustrated but at the same time understanding her point. He couldn't not admire her patriotism. "I'm not asking you to give up everything. We'll visit as often as you'd like. Is there no room in your plans for happy accidents?"

He held his breath for the answer but kept digging. He couldn't afford to stop, not for a second. It could all come down to the wire. When Darek came for them in the morning, he didn't plan on still being here.

"You're so not a *happy accident,*" she countered from above. "You're too much. Larger-than-life. Overwhelming. A little scary. Very pushy. To the point of arrogant."

"Right. You might have mentioned that already. But we worked once."

Silence.

He needed to press his point, but pressed his lips together instead. He didn't want to badger her. She had enough stress on her shoulders at the moment. They would survive this, and he would have more time, other opportunities to convince her that he was the only man for her.

"Please rest," he told her again. "At least lie down on the bed and take the weight off your feet. Maybe you'll fall asleep."

"I doubt that." Her voice sounded strained when

she responded after a second. "I'm having more cramps."

His muscles clenched. He dug faster. "Practice contractions again?"

She stayed silent.

He did stop then and stepped over so he was under the hole that led up to the shack, but he couldn't see her. She was probably on the bed. "Isabelle?"

"I think I'm having the baby."

Chapter Eleven

"Do you need me to come up?" Adrenaline rushed through Amir's veins. He wouldn't allow fear. He'd been trained to keep his head under pressure, an attribute drilled into him at an early age, part of his education as the future leader of his country.

"I'm fine. Just hurry so you can get us out of here," Isabelle told him.

He blinked against the dust that hung in the air, spit the taste of dirt from his mouth, but didn't stop working. He dug like he'd never dug before, which wasn't saying much, since, as a prince, he hadn't done all that much digging.

Except that time when he'd attempted to climb Mount Everest with a group of daredevil friends of his. An avalanche buried them, and he'd been one of the lucky ones, reaching the surface first. He and a friend had dug like fiends to get to the rest of the team. Everyone made it out alive without serious injury, save for a broken collarbone and a broken leg.

Now it was Isabelle who was in trouble, and he found that he was a hundred times as willing to fight for her. He ignored the pain in his shoulder. He slammed the screwdriver into the hardened soil, loosened a chunk, then removed it, moving on to the next, then the next.

Before he'd come back to Wyoming, he'd thought his wild adventure days were over. But with Isabelle and his son depending on him, the stakes were higher than ever. All he wanted now was to see them safe. Adventure was way overrated. He would never again miss the bulls in Spain.

Minutes ticked by and turned into hours. As best he could tell. He could only guess at the passage of time down there in the darkness.

"How do you feel now?" he called up, pausing only for a second to wipe the sweat from his forehead, then going back to the work.

"Contractions are still almost twenty minutes or so apart. Stop asking. I'll let you know when there's something for you to be nervous about."

Sheiks didn't get nervous, he scoffed. He was… justifiably concerned. His princess was having a baby. In America. In a shed. Without the royal physician, without any of the royal court attending. They were breaking so many protocols, but he couldn't even think of that. She was in pain. Not all the time, but periodically. He could hear it in her voice. According to her, the contractions were twenty minutes apart. Whatever that meant.

He needed to get her out of here. First, he needed

to find the end of this tunnel and clear the exit, then he needed to widen the hole in the floor so she would fit through it.

He worked as hard as he could, stopped to check on her, then went back to work again. The night moved along, time running out.

Then half the wall that blocked the tunnel came down at last, not enough for him to crawl through yet, but enough to see all that dark, promising space behind it. He grabbed the screwdriver and went back to work. "Are you still all right?"

"Are you digging or worrying?"

"I'm not worried. I just don't want you to worry," he told her, worried through and through that she'd been right and he couldn't protect her, after all.

"Oh, God."

"What? What is it?" He was ready to climb up to her.

"I just realized that even if we get out, we'll have to walk miles and miles to civilization."

"I'll come up with something." There was an SUV out there, plus the black van. His muscles clenched when he heard the hiss of her breathing.

"Okay. I'm going to trust you on this," she said after a long moment.

Trust. "Why now?"

"Because I don't have any other choice. Because I can't do this alone." She groaned.

"Are you in pain?"

"I'm good," she told him.

He didn't believe her for a second.

SHE WAS HEALTHY. The baby was healthy. The ob-gyn had predicted a normal, uneventful labor. Isabelle hoped Dr. Szunoman was right, because as of now, it sure didn't look like they were going to make it to the hospital.

Night had fallen. Hours had passed.

Her contractions were ten minutes apart.

Her labor wasn't exactly progressing with the speed of light. At the hospital they might have tried to hurry it along chemically, but under the circumstances she was more than grateful for her tardy baby.

Amir came up from the hidey-hole, covered in dust. "The way is clear all the way to the end. The tunnel goes on for about fifty feet, but the exit is sealed. How do you feel?" He brushed off his hair and shirt.

"Like a woman in labor." She was lying on her side, rubbing her lower back to ease her muscles. When she'd first seen the bed, she wouldn't have touched it with a ten-foot pole. She wasn't so picky now. She was just glad it held her weight.

Amir dusted himself off one more time, stomping his feet quietly to get the dirt off his shoes. "May I?"

He lay silently next to her so they were facing each other and pressed his hands next to hers, searching out the stiffest muscles. His long fingers worked miracles. When the next contraction came, it passed a lot more smoothly.

He kissed her forehead. "How much time do we have?"

"I would guess several hours. But it's not an exact science."

She let her body relax against his. True, they hadn't known each other long, but he'd never felt like a stranger to her, not even at the beginning. From the first look that passed between them, the connection had been undeniable.

She moved closer and placed her head on his shoulder. They lay there, side by side, their heartbeats synchronizing. Then he pressed another kiss on top of her head. "I should go back to work."

"You need to rest. If you overtax your system, you can fall right back into a coma. That happens more than you think." In fact, he was putting his health at serious risk with all this exertion. "How is the bullet hole?"

"Nothing to worry about."

"You're taking this too lightly."

"I hate being this weak. It's going infuriatingly slow down there. I push as hard as I can, but the progress is not as rapid as it should be." His voice was tight, frustration clearly taking its toll on him.

"I suppose that conflicts with your macho sheik self-image. You don't have to be as strong as a comic-book hero, you know. It's already a miracle that you're still standing."

A brooding look came into his dark eyes. "I have to be…everything. I'm the leader of my country. People look to me for leadership and security." He said the words with a heavy heart, not in a way a power-hungry man who reveled in his position would have. There was a marked difference between him and Darek, whose only motivation seemed to be greed.

Amir was a man of honor, but a man of contradictions, too. He was exotic, powerful, even in recovery, since his power did not come only from muscles. He had strength of character…. Isabelle cut that train of thought off, recognizing the slippery slope ahead of her. Admire him too much, desire him too much, and the next thing she knew, she would be falling in love with him. Not if she could help it. She looked away.

"You shouldn't fight this," he said, as if reading her mind.

She didn't have a chance to disagree with him. Her muscles clenched. The next contraction was starting. Oh, man. This was so not how she had planned this. She wanted one of those comfortable hospital beds. She wanted nurses. She wanted ice chips, for heaven's sake.

Then Amir took her hand, and she found that all she really needed was him.

HE HELD HER through the contraction, drawing soothing circles on her belly. He wanted to stay with her until she felt better, but knew she wouldn't truly feel better until his son was born, and things would get a lot more difficult between now and then. He didn't want his heir to be born in this shack. So after staying with her for a few more contractions, and after he had a chance to rest a little, he returned to work in the tunnel.

"You know, I have assisted at birthing several times," he called back as he picked up the screwdriver.

"You have?" Hope rang in her voice.

"Certainly." He felt much better for having thought of that. "From an early age. I've helped with the birthing of my father's prize Arabian horses at the royal stables."

She grunted and mumbled something that sounded like "Thanks for nothing." But he must have misunderstood that. His knowledge of the mechanics was a good thing.

But plan A was still to get her out of here and get her to the nearest hospital or clinic.

He dug until his fingertips bled. He couldn't see them; he only felt the wetness. He was in a hole underground in the middle of the night. He was going by feel. He fought for every single inch, blocking the pain in his arms and legs, in his back. He didn't care if he fell back into a bloody coma, as long as it didn't happen until after he had gotten Isabelle to safety.

Nothing beyond Isabelle and his son mattered.

"Are you still feeling okay?" He made sure to ask every few minutes.

"Let me know if you come across an epidural kit."

He could hear the pain in her voice. He dug harder.

"Someone's coming," she hissed.

He ran for the hole and lunged up. He was half in, half out of it when Darek burst in.

The man's gun came up immediately. "What are you doing?"

"Found a hole down there. Just looking around, that's all." Amir pushed himself up all the way, keeping his voice steady. "Nothing helpful, unfortunately."

"I have a plan!" Darek shouted, his stance full of menace. "If you mess it up, you are not going to like what happens next." He walked over, crouched without moving the gun from Amir and glanced down.

"Relax. There's no exit," Amir told him.

"Or there is," he said, "but she couldn't go down and you wouldn't leave her. How touching." He stood and walked back to the door, where Amir couldn't lunge at him as easily. "Just think, not long now and you'll be together for all eternity."

THE NEXT CONTRACTION came and took Isabelle's breath away. She stifled a gasp. Amir must have heard it, anyway, because he glanced at her, shaking his head nearly imperceptibly. He didn't want her to draw attention to herself, and she was fine with that. She'd already decided to hide her labor from their captors. Now that they had Amir, they didn't really need her for anything. If she became too much trouble, the easiest thing for them was just to finish her off right here.

Darek was handing a phone to Amir. "Call Efraim. Time to set up our little meeting."

Anger and tension rolled off Amir in waves, but he dialed.

"You tell him you're trapped at the old county airfield. Tell him to trust no outsiders. Insist that the princes come alone to help you." Darek paused. "Tell him you're injured."

"It's Amir," he said when the call was picked up. "Anybody else there beyond the four of you? Good." Then he repeated the message Darek had demanded he relay. He finished with, "Trust no one outside that room. Do you hear me? You should all come, but no one else. Nobody else can be trusted."

Then Darek took the phone away from him, closed it, shoved it back into his pocket. "I do like it when a plan comes together, even if it comes together a month late. You should have all died in that car explosion. You would have if I had been the one to set the charges. It's difficult to find good hired help," he taunted them. "I should have known and come to take care of everything on my own in the first place. It's more satisfactory like this, anyway."

"Why didn't you?" Amir asked, probably stalling for time.

"I thought your death being linked back to me would be less likely if we weren't on the same continent when the tragedy happened."

"And now?"

"And now I think getting you out of the way is worth the risk. I've waited a long time for this."

Amir shuffled to the side little by little, getting as far away from her as he could. And while she wished for nothing more than the comfort his arms could give, she understood that he was doing this to keep Darek's gun pointed away from her.

He thought Darek would shoot now. The realization hit her and took her breath away. Amir had called the others. The trap was now set. Did that make him disposable? She felt for the empty bottle, her only weapon. Last she'd seen it, it was by the foot of the bed.

She was not going to go out like this. She kept her eyes on Amir, waiting for him to give some sort of a signal. They had no choice but to attack now. He had to see that.

But instead of going for Darek's throat, Amir said, "Five foreign princes murdered. You know there'll be a thorough international investigation. This is not something you can sweep under the carpet."

"What murder? The five royals will board a private chopper at an abandoned airstrip to avoid the media. A day of aerial sightseeing that will end in tragedy. The chopper will plunge to a fiery death. If the investigation finds any evidence of tampering, the xenophobic, foreign-hating protesters will be blamed. How fortunate that the media featured them so prominently," he said slyly, as if he had something to do with that.

She couldn't care less about his gloating. She was just grateful that he hadn't started shooting yet. She pressed her lips together as the next contraction came. She stood as still as she could, leaning against the bed and holding her breath.

Then he stepped back out the door and motioned with his gun for them to follow. "We better get to the airfield. The back road is all washed out, according to my local friends. Getting there might take us a while. And you know how I hate to be late. Punctuality is the courtesy of kings, as they say."

Okay, baby. Not yet. Please wait a little longer. I can be very grateful for favors. Ask any of my friends. I'm thinking puppy.

The baby kicked.

"Leave Isabelle here. She has nothing to do with this," Amir insisted. "Nobody but the other four royals know that she's carrying my child. She refused to marry me. She doesn't want her son to have anything to do with me or Jamala. They'll be no threat to you."

Sweat rolled down her forehead. Where was an air-conditioned delivery room when you needed one? And where were the drugs, most importantly?

"Indeed not." Darek sneered. "Because I'm going to tie up all loose ends. But I'm not completely unfair. Khalid blood might make it to your throne if your sister plays her cards right. After consoling the proud Saida in her grief over your death, I might just marry her as my second wife. My son will be your nephew. And after my death, Jamala's throne will be his. You must admit, it's a certain kind of justice. For our friendship's sake."

Amir stood tall. "You are a disgrace to everything that is honorable."

The pain that held Isabelle tight intensified. A gasp escaped her lips. Her hands flew up to her abdomen. *Not yet. Please.*

"Is she in labor?" Darek turned to her. "She better not slow us down. Having her body found in the wreckage is not imperative. She could always just disappear. As you said, nobody would connect her to you, would they?"

Chapter Twelve

The men outside were getting into their vehicles.

"How long does labor last?" Amir asked Isabelle, standing as close to her as possible, an arm around her waist, helping her to hold herself up.

Darek was arguing with the men, swearing at them for something, paying no attention.

"Average first labor? Anywhere from twelve hours to twenty-four. Or it could go on for days."

He felt the blood run out of his face.

"I don't think mine will," she told him. "Everything seems to be progressing. Contractions are ten minutes apart."

"I apologize." Whether she blamed him or not, this was all his fault.

"We don't have time for apologies." She breathed loudly.

"If I knew there would be any danger to you...." He'd come to Wyoming with distinct plans for Isabelle, but those fantasies didn't look anything like this. He had hoped for a couple of days together.

Days of passion once again, but longer this time, maybe a week or even more.

He brushed his free hand over the screwdriver in the waist of his trousers, in the back, making sure his shirt fully covered it. "I've been a fool."

Her gaze searched his. "For coming back to Wyoming? Not like you knew that you'd be attacked here. We're not exactly a hotbed of criminal activity. I don't think anything like this has ever happened in Dumont."

He didn't have time to waste. Whatever he wanted to tell her had to be said now, in case they didn't have time later. "I'm a fool for not realizing right away that I wanted you forever. I should have known nine months ago. I should have searched you out right after you left that morning. I wasted all this time." His hands fisted.

Ever since he'd gotten off the plane, things had gone from bad to worse. First the limousine blowing up; Bahur, his guard who drove the car, dying; him going into a coma. Which drew Isabelle into the circle of danger. And now his friends were headed into an ambush.

If any one of them died, it would devastate COIN. If all of them died, it would destabilize the region, and their countries would suffer for years, if not decades, in the ensuing power struggle.

Had Efraim understood his hints? When he'd asked who was in the room, Efraim had listed the four royals, plus Jake Wolf and Wade. *You should all come, but no one else,* he'd told Efraim. So six would come instead of the four, Darek expected. *Trust no one outside that room.* He hoped they understood that meant Darek, the only one of their circle who hadn't been in the room at the time.

"When we are in the car, I'm going to distract them. I'll take out as many as I can. No matter what happens to me, you grab the steering wheel and drive away as fast as you're able."

"Because I look like I would enjoy a car race right about now?" She was gasping for air.

"Because you look like you would do anything to have our son born in safety."

She held his gaze for a long time; then she nodded, a single tear rolling down her face. "Our chances are not too good, are they?"

"I would have loved you. We would have had a good marriage." He didn't have time to say more.

Darek was turning to them, grabbing Isabelle's arm to drag her after him.

"Out to the SUV." His free hand held the gun on Isabelle. He knew he could keep Amir in line by threatening her.

Four other men stood around the two vehicles. Three of them had come with Darek; the fourth was their initial kidnapper.

One of the men shoved Amir into the back of the SUV; another tried to do the same with Isabelle.

"Let her sit in the front," Amir told Darek. "At least let her be comfortable as long as she can be."

A sneer crept onto the man's face.

"You will have a wife someday," Amir told him. "We were friends once."

"So long ago I can barely remember," Darek said but then nodded toward Isabelle, and the man holding her arm helped her into the front passenger seat before going around and sitting behind the wheel.

The other two men got into the back, bracketing Amir on each side. Darek went to ride in the black van.

"How far is it to the airport?" Amir asked the men when they started rolling.

"An hour, I guess. Anxious to die, Sheik?"

BREATHE DEEP. BREATHE evenly. Easier said than done. Isabelle braced one hand against the dashboard, trying to cope as best she could, which wasn't going well. The baby was coming. She had to watch for some sort of a sign from Amir, at which point he would fight off the men while she drove away. *Right.* Was he insane?

But they had to do *something.*

He was not going to take out three armed men alone. Which meant that she had to take out the driver. She was closest to the man, so it was the only logical thing. Could she do it? Could she really kill a man in the middle of labor? It went against the whole "bringing new life into the world" theme of the moment.

And even if she did, and Amir handled the other two—that "if" being the size of Bow Mountain—there was the small matter of the black van driving ahead of them on the narrow road. She had no way of passing. Which meant she would somehow have to turn the SUV around and drive off in the opposite direction.

Sure. That would happen.

Except that it had to happen. *Deep breath.* Because she was *not* going to die today. She was going to give birth to her son, keep him safe, and she was not going to let the bastards have Amir, either. She didn't know when it happened, she didn't know whether she liked that it had happened, but she was pretty sure she was falling in love with the man, God help her.

He wanted to protect her and stand by her side and all that nonsense, and she was barely freaked out by the thought anymore. It was official. Pregnancy hormones did give her brain damage.

She gritted her teeth as a contraction came. Squeezed her eyes shut. *Breathe.* The pain got worse with each contraction. She handled it. Then the long, agonizing seconds were over at last, and her focus had to be back on their current situation again.

They drove through a wooded area, came out into an open field, scaring a couple of grazing antelope into the bush. But soon they were in the woods again. The black van got farther ahead of them, then disappeared around a bend.

"Now," Amir said at the same time as he went for the screwdriver at his back with his right hand and stabbed it into the throat of the man who sat on his right. With his left he punched the driver hard in the temple. Then, almost simultaneously, he plowed into the man on his left, reached for the door handle and shoved the door open, causing both of them to tumble from the vehicle.

"Amir!" She slammed her elbow into the driver's face with all her strength, then grabbed the gun from his lap, her mind struggling to catch up with what had just happened.

Driving from the passenger seat with her left hand was no picnic, especially since she was watching in the rearview mirror as Amir wrestled in the middle of the road, fighting for his life. He wasn't going to last long. He was still too weak.

And he had to have known that, too, must have known all along while he made and executed his crazy plan. He had prepared to die so she could get away.

Blazing buzzards.

She aimed the gun at the driver, who was reviving and was trying to grab her. The mother of all contractions ripped through her. "Make my day," she said to the man through clenched teeth.

Probably didn't look too pretty, but it proved to be effective. The man assessed his situation correctly and took his foot off the gas, then jumped from the car as it slowed. Good riddance.

The giant SUV had enough room in the front for her to slide over. The black van was still out of sight up ahead. She made a shaky three-point turn as soon as the contraction passed, was ready to run the man over if he stood in her way, but he wasn't that dumb.

She sped by him, going back for Amir.

He was off the road, rolling in the dirt by a stand of bushes, Darek's man on top of him.

She put the car in park. Slid out. Stopped for a second to breathe hard. When the pain in her side passed, she marched up to the men and put her gun to the idiot's head. "Let him go."

The guy looked at her but didn't seem to believe her.

"So help me God, I will shoot you dead right now, right here. I'm a pregnant woman in labor. Do I look like I'm kidding?"

It was enough to make him hesitate. Which was enough for Amir to punch him and roll out from under him. He grabbed after Amir, so she shot in the general direction of the guy. He took the hint, pushed to his feet and started running toward his buddy.

"Get in the car." Amir grabbed her elbow and tried to drag her after him, but he was pretty beaten up, so it wasn't immediately obvious who was dragging whom. "You shouldn't have stopped. You could be a mile down the road by now."

"You shouldn't have planned a suicide mission. How could you? You are the father of my son!" She climbed in, holding her belly. "You ask me to marry you and then you try to get yourself killed? What kind of a follow-through is that?" She was yelling, anger furrowing her brows, but deep inside she was so relieved she could have cried. They'd gotten away.

The man Amir had stabbed in the throat had bled to death and Amir shoved the body out of the back, then jumped in behind the steering wheel. "You don't want to marry me, anyway," he reminded her as he put his foot on the gas and the SUV shot forward.

"I can change my mind. It's every woman's prerogative around here."

He flashed her a surprised look while the car gathered speed. "Have you?"

"Not yet, but maybe I will. You're not going find out if by the time I make up my mind, you're dead!" Another contraction was coming. She was running out of breath.

He was grinning like an idiot.

Then the black van slammed into them, jarring her so hard her teeth rattled. Thank God she'd had the presence of mind to put on her seat belt. She craned her neck, then bit her lip in despair. Their enemies were right at their back.

"Go faster!"

"I can't." Amir's face darkened. "They busted one of the back tires."

Again, they were bumped. She held her belly. Being jiggled hurt like hell. "I don't know what this is doing to the baby." She cried out in pain when the next jostle came. "Make them stop." She didn't want to think what might happen if she hit her stomach.

Amir held her gaze for a long moment. Then

he took his foot off the gas pedal and put it on the brake. He threw the gun out the window so the men behind them could see it.

"Where are the other two guns?" Darek shouted.

"I don't have those. I swear. We surrender." Amir opened the door and got out, his hands in the air.

And just like that, their brief flight to freedom was over.

THEY WERE STRAPPED in the back of a chopper. Isabelle's contractions were five minutes apart. Amir was no expert, but he was pretty sure that meant the baby could come very soon now.

Darek was with them, more of his men hidden around the abandoned airstrip. A cloud of dust was coming closer and closer. The royals were arriving in two separate vehicles.

"Wait." Amir wiggled his hand, trying to loosen the ropes that bound his wrists to the armrests. "You should have my signet ring. If Saida ever does have a son, I want him to have it. It's been in the family for generations."

Darek shrugged and came over.

Amir bent his finger slightly so that the ring wouldn't come off so easily. Darek had to put the gun down so he could hang on to Amir's hand with one hand and tug the ring with the other, probably wanting that symbol of Jamalan royal power for himself.

What he wanted didn't matter. The only thing

that mattered was that he was close enough at last, within reach.

Now. Amir slammed his forehead into Darek's with all the strength he had left. Pain reverberated through his skull. For a second, he saw double.

"You…" Darek blinked hard, faltered, dealing with the impact in his own way.

Outside, the royals' vehicles were coming to a stop. It would all be over within minutes.

Darek lifted his hand. He was going to shoot.

Amir lurched against his restraints. Growled when he couldn't break free.

But instead of shooting, Darek collapsed to one knee. This was it. Their last chance. Amir kicked him in the head, using whatever strength he had left. And at last, the man folded.

"Watch out! Watch out! It's a trap!" Amir shouted but wasn't sure whether he could be heard outside the chopper.

"It's a trap!" Isabelle added her voice to his, screaming at the top of her lungs, using the pain of her labor as inspiration, because she way outdid him.

Darek's gun lay on the floor, inches from Amir's feet. He stretched to drag it closer with his foot, then kicked his shoe off, guided the weapon up his leg with his toes until he could reach it with his fingertips.

"Got it," he grunted to Isabelle, who stopped screaming.

"Watch out!"

Darek was reviving, lunging for him.

With his hand tied, aiming correctly was impossible, but he emptied the magazine in the general direction, hitting Darek in the hip by pure chance and sending him sprawling back. Not as satisfactory as a clean kill, but at least the gunfire would definitely tip off his friends to trouble.

Gunfire erupted outside, too.

Isabelle moaned, drawing his attention.

"Can you hold on a little longer?"

Her eyes were closed as she focused on her breathing, a sheen of sweat covering her forehead. "Three minutes apart."

"Coming on board," a voice shouted from outside.

Jake Wolf was the first onto the chopper. Took in Darek. "I knew something wasn't right with him." He pulled a knife from his belt and cut Isabelle's ropes first, then Amir's, handing him a gun at the same time.

Which he tried to use to finish off Darek.

"No." Jake knocked his hand aside. "The law will take care of him."

"He wanted to force Saida to become his second wife after we were all dead." Amir hissed the words just as Darek rose somehow and pulled another gun from behind his back.

Two shots went off at the same time as Isabelle screamed in pain.

One hit Darek in the head; one in the heart.

Amir and Jake exchanged glances, then moved to help Isabelle out of the chopper.

Efraim got on board, filling what little space was left. "Everyone all right?"

"We need to get her to a hospital." Amir swore under his breath when he realized he was too weak to help. His shoulder wound had reopened at one point during the fight. He'd lost enough blood to feel the difference.

"You're needed out there," Efraim told Jake, sending him on his way. Then he turned to Isabelle. "I'm Sheik Efraim. I apologize for the informality, madam." He lifted her into his arms swiftly, then headed for the exit. "I'll try not to jostle you. But when one of the bullets that are flying outside hits the fuel tank, we don't want to be in here," he told her.

Amir hurried after them, wholeheartedly agreeing.

Efraim paused at the door, pulled back so Amir could shoot the man who was aiming right at them. The first bullet missed, but the second found its target and the guy running toward the chopper fell with a cry.

Amir jumped to the ground first, covering Efraim, who had his hands full with Isabelle. A part of him hated the sight of her in another man's arms, but he had to accept that Ephraim was stronger and could move faster.

And speed was imperative, since they were in the middle of an old-fashioned Western shoot-out, people running and ducking, bullets coming from every direction. For a second, he couldn't even tell how the battle was going, who was winning.

"Go!" He covered Efraim, the three of them heading as best they could for the cars. He felt civility melt off him, the restraint he had adopted since he'd become ruler of his country. The warrior blood of his ancestors rushed in his veins. Savagery filled him and he embraced it. He would not let her be harmed. Not if he had to die for her safety.

Protect mine. Kill the enemy.

They were out in the open, but there was no help for it. Staying in the chopper was too dangerous. Once they were in the car, they could get out of there and head to the nearest hospital.

"Watch out!" Wade, his half-brother, shouted, popping up from behind cover.

"How did he get here?"

"He came to the resort after he heard on the news that you were found. Of course, by then you'd disappeared again," Efraim said.

Some of the bullets came so close that at one point he was certain Efraim had been hit. But no, his friend kept on going. For how long? The cars were a good hundred yards away, on open land. He shot at every position that shot at them, trying to keep them down, going for a head shot if he had a chance.

But, too soon, he ran out of bullets.

This was it; this was the end. Enraged, he threw the empty gun toward the enemy, and bolted forward, ready for hand-to-hand combat if needed, unable to accept that he couldn't do more, that he might not be able to save his son and Isabelle, the woman he was in love with.

Then Wade and his friends were rushing out of cover and up to him, tossing him a fresh weapon, forming a circle around Isabelle and defending her with their lives.

Chapter Thirteen

Had she ever said that she didn't want a powerful man to protect her? Had she been that stupid? She was ready for all the protection of the fighting royals now and then some. In fact, if anyone wanted to send in the National Guard, she would be very grateful.

The royals were moving her toward a waiting car. One of the men by her side fell, but more of the enemy was killed or injured. Fresh gunfire sounded in the distance.

"Who," she gasped, "are they?" There better not be more of Darek's men coming.

"Backup," one of the royals told her. We knew something wasn't right when Amir called. "We have enough loyal people left that between them and Jake Wolf's men, we have the airfield surrounded."

"The fight ends here today," Efraim said darkly. "There won't be any *live to fight another day*."

Endless seconds passed before Darek's men realized that the boss wasn't coming out of the chopper and they were trapped. Then chaos erupted.

They didn't know which way to run, and some ran straight into bullet fire. She barely registered all that, could barely follow the battle. Her contractions couldn't be more than a minute apart now. The baby was coming.

Finally, they reached the car and she was helped into the back. She sat sideways so she could put up her feet. Amir jumped into the driver's seat. Another royal, Prince Stefan, if she was correct, got in next to him in the front, providing cover.

"Go!" Efraim slapped the roof. "We can handle the rest here."

Then they were flying.

She noted little of the landscape that whizzed by them. She focused inward and did her breathing.

By the time they reached Dumont General, she was feeling the urge to push. She held it back. "Just a few more minutes, baby. We're almost ready," she whispered to her belly. "Go to the ambulance bay," she told Amir.

The guys there would have her on a gurney and wheeled up to Labor and Delivery before anyone could blink. Except, several ambulances blocked the ambulance bay, the area a beehive of activity, people rushing around. Had to have been a major accident somewhere. *Oh, God.*

"Employee entrance." She moaned in pain as she pointed.

That was the closest door to them now and would get her to her destination faster than going back around to any of the main entrances.

One of the pulmonary nurses was coming out just as Amir parked. Prince Stefan lifted Isabelle out of the car.

The nurse recognized her and held the door open for them. "Oh, yea, congratulations! Looks like this is your big day." Then she took in their grim faces and the blood that covered Amir's shoulder and grew uncertain. "Is everything all right here?"

"The baby is coming." Isabelle gritted out the words.

The nurse was pulling out her cell phone. "I'll call ahead and let them know."

They sailed right by her.

Prince Stefan ran forward until Amir miraculously produced a gurney from one of the side hallways. She felt marginally better when she was finally lying flat on her back.

"Straight ahead," she told them.

The farther down the corridor they got, the more people they had to go around.

"Out of the way!" Prince Stefan tried to clear the corridor and did a pretty good job of it.

"The future queen of Jamala is having my heir. I demand assistance immediately!" Amir bellowed, making heads turn.

Then they were in a gallery above a waiting area, at the elevator bank. Only three elevator stops from Labor and Delivery.

"We're going up. Third floor," Prince Stefan said, reading the directory, jabbing the button repeatedly.

Amir held her hand. "Are you in much pain?"

Did doughnuts stick to women's hips? But she wasn't as worried about the pain as she was about her son. The last two days had been crazy with all the stress and running for their lives. She just wanted her baby to arrive safely and be healthy.

Amir was looking at her with turmoil on his face, uncertainty in his dark eyes for the first time since she'd known him.

"What is it? Spit it out, for heaven's sake." She was low on patience at the minute.

"I don't want my son born a bastard," he said in a tone of urgency.

Her first inclination was to hit him over the head with the nearest IV stand, but since none were within reach, she simply gritted her teeth. "Now is so not the best time to go medieval on me."

But as she looked into his turbulent dark eyes, she realized suddenly what this meant to him. *This* was what he believed in. This was right and important to him, a part of his honor, which was the core of the man, like being American and an independent woman was the core of her.

"All right." She couldn't believe she was saying this. "Okay."

His face lit up with triumph; then his gaze settled on the sign on the door of the nearby hospital chaplain's office. He grabbed the gurney and pushed her forward.

Unbelievable.

"I'll hold on for five more minutes, but then I

don't care if a meteor the size of Bow Mountain hits the hospital. I *will* start pushing."

He didn't say anything. He was too busy grinning.

Prince Stefan was dragging the priest out before they reached the door.

"I cannot do this," Father Francis was protesting. "I cannot officiate a Catholic wedding between two people who are not Catholic, as I told Prince Stefan here. And there's a waiting period. Then there's the matter of a marriage license. It's impossible. It's not up to me, my children."

Amir gave the man the glare of death. But before he could do more, the elevator dinged and he raced back there with her.

"I need to get married in the next five minutes," she told one of the orderlies who got on with them at the last second. "Any suggestions here?"

"There's a rabbi on the ninth floor, but he's out of it. He just came out of surgery. He won't be coming around anytime soon."

"How about someone who got some license over the internet?" She was desperate and nearly blind with pain.

The orderly nodded. "I got a cousin like that in Jersey."

Might as well be on the moon.

Then they were on the third floor and rushing down the corridor, passing by the Labor and Delivery Unit's large lounge, where family members were allowed to wait. The place was full of people, some pacing, some guzzling coffee, some sleeping on chairs that had been pushed together.

Amir stopped the gurney. "I, Sheik Amir Khalid, marry this woman, Isabelle Andrews, and take her as my one and only wife in love, to cherish and protect forever," he announced boldly to the room.

In love...

Her heart nearly stopped beating as people stared at them wide-eyed.

"I, Prince Stefan Lutece, witness this."

Then they were moving again.

The urge to bear down was irresistible. "What was that?"

"A traditional, centuries-old Jamalan wedding ceremony," said Amir.

"But I didn't say anything."

"It's not necessary. I announced and Stefan witnessed. We are now married."

There were so many things wrong with that, she couldn't even begin to list them, and she didn't want to at the moment. Nurses descended on her, and someone paged Dr. Szunoman, who was still on call, thank heavens.

When they began to undress her, the two men backed out of the room, thankfully. She was given a hospital gown, and her legs were put in stirrups. She was barely hooked up to the monitors when she started pushing.

Amir came back in, dressed in scrubs, Dr. Szunoman right behind him. "I hear it's time. How are you doing, Isabelle?"

"Bursting."

"It'll be over soon. Push with each contraction. Rest in between." He situated himself on a stool.

Amir took her hand. "I love you."

His cheeks grew slightly pink at the public admission. She had a hunch Jamalan sheiks weren't quite so free about displaying their feelings in public, but at the moment it was the exact thing she needed to hear.

"I love you, too."

"The head is crowning," Dr. Szunoman piped in.

The baby's nurse came in. At Dumont General, they had separate nurses for the mother and the baby, a practice that could save lives during a difficult delivery.

"One big push," the doctor said, encouraging her.

It was the best and the worst day of her life at the same time. She felt as if her body was being torn in two, and part of her was certain that she was dying.

She pushed with all her heart, squeezing Amir's hand for all she was worth.

"The head is free."

She felt tears filling her eyes.

"One more big push."

She pushed and she screamed.

"Congratulations. You have a bouncing baby boy," the doctor said, then announced the time of birth as he laid her precious son on her chest.

She looked into the most beautiful face she'd ever seen, at dark eyes and dark hair, a chin that was a miniature version of Amir's. Her tears were now freely flowing. "Oh, baby." He was the most beautiful thing she'd ever seen.

"I love you so much," she whispered to her son. "And I love you, too." She looked up at Amir, whose eyes were glistening suspiciously.

Time to complete their wedding. Her way.

"I, Isabelle Andrews, take you, Sheik Amir Khalid, as my husband in love." She looked at Dr. Szunoman. "Say you witness."

The doctor gave her a confused look but said, "I witness."

Warmth spread through her, and she felt endless love for the two men in her life, both of them a miracle in their own way. She took Amir's hand and placed it gently on the baby's back. "This is Amir, your daddy. I'm Isabelle, your mommy." Then she added, "Your friends can call me Mrs. Sheik."

Chapter Fourteen

Six weeks later

Amazing what a motivated group of knowledge-able people could accomplish in six weeks, Isabelle thought as she looked out from the balcony of the splendidly decorated palace. In the distance shone the brilliant azure of the Mediterranean Sea. In the square in front of the palace, a sea of eager faces had gathered for the royal wedding.

The make-haste vows at the hospital were sufficient, but since Amir was the sheik, his station demanded that a larger ceremony also be performed. And he gave his people what they wanted. Isabelle's head was still buzzing from the events of the day.

The party was just getting started below, exotic music and laughter filling the air. Nearby, on a smaller balcony, Antoine and Beth were doing some heavy-duty kissing. One floor up, she could see Stefan and Jane doing the same. All of Amir's friends were there with their future brides. Hers was only the first in a string of expected royal weddings.

The whole world was talking about the series of royal nuptials. Tourism was booming, which was an unexpected bonus on top of the sizable funds the princes' U.S. summit had brought in.

She spotted Amir on the main patio with Saida and Wade, the three deep in conversation. The pleasure of having his family together was visible on Amir's face even from this distance. Saida had her arm linked through Wade's. She was making up for lost time, getting to know her half-brother. Isabelle heard plenty of stories, since Saida was quickly becoming her best friend, advising her on the wedding and stopping in several times a day to play with the baby. She was the best aunt ever.

Jake Wolf leaned against the balustrade a few yards back, waiting patiently for his future bride to finish saying good-night to her brothers so he could take her up to their suite. The two were made for each other, Isabelle thought, and grinned. She was happier than she'd ever been and sharing that happiness with others made everything even better.

She caught sight of Sebastian dancing with Jessica as if she were the only woman in the world. The heat between those two was palpable. Not far from them, Efraim was through dancing, swept Callie into his arms and carried her off the dance floor, heading toward the palace like a caravan bandit carrying his prize. Callie threw her arms around his neck as she laughed with pleasure.

Isabelle went back inside her lavish room, crossed the floor to one of the side doors and checked in on Akif, the best little baby in the world, who slept peacefully in the nursery. They had named him after Amir's grandfather, a popular decision that was celebrated by the whole country.

The guards were giving formal greetings outside in the hallway, their voices drawing her attention. Amir was coming.

As always, he came straight to their son, wrapping his arms around Isabelle from behind, kissing the top of her head as they looked together at their softly sleeping baby.

"I just got news that the last of Darek's men has been rounded up," Amir said after a long moment. "Even the Russian connection."

She knew Amir could protect their family, but knowing for sure that all danger had ended erased even her last few worries.

Then he turned her in his arms. "Did the ceremony tire you out?" Flames of desire burned in his gaze.

Muscles clenched low in her belly. "It was amazing." Thousands of years of tradition. A hundred thousand people cheering her name. Now that it was over, it seemed even more unreal, as if she'd dreamt the whole thing.

"You are amazing." Amir lowered his head, settling his lips over hers softly.

Her body didn't even try to fight the onslaught

of sensations; it capitulated immediately. She put a hand on his chest and gave herself over to the kiss.

She heated through to the core, got lost in pleasure, still amazed at how easy this was, after all, how right it felt. Now that her life had been tied to his twice, she didn't feel powerless, as she had feared. She didn't feel lost or diminished. She felt exactly right, content and deliriously happy.

She gave a reluctant moan when he stepped away, then frowned when she saw that his lips were pressed together tightly, his hands slipping away from her.

"I wish…" He paused. "I apologize for my impatience. When you're ready."

And she figured out at last what he was talking about. "The royal physician stopped by to see me yesterday."

Immediately he frowned. "Are you sick?"

"I'm…" She cleared her throat. "I'm fully recovered from childbirth."

"Excellent." His frown lines eased. Then hope replaced worry in his eyes as realization dawned on him. "Are you recovered *all* the way?"

She smiled and bit her lower lip, feeling ridiculously shy all of a sudden. She couldn't even say the word. She simply nodded.

"And do you feel…" Now he seemed at a loss for words.

"Yes." She wanted him so much she was going to die if he didn't touch her in the next five seconds.

"Yes as in…"

She closed the distance between them and pressed her lips against his.

That was all the hint he needed.

The next second she was in his arms and he was striding back to their suite with her, to the sprawling bed where they had spent every single night together since arriving in Jamala, sleeping in each other's arms.

Something told her the innocence of mere sleep was officially over. Every cell in her body thrilled.

He lowered her to her feet and reached for the top button of the richly embroidered golden gown she had worn for the wedding, according to Jalaman tradition. Their second wedding had been a fairy-tale fantasy. And it only kept getting better.

She sighed when the material finally gave and Amir cupped her breast. She tugged to get completely out of the gown, but Amir's free hand stayed in hers.

"There is no hurry."

Right. She relaxed into his embrace. They had their whole lives together. She barely dared thinking about that, unsure if she deserved this much happiness.

His hot lips trailed from her lips to her neck, sending delicious shivers through her.

His fingers kept on working the gown, finishing with the buttons at last and pushing the brocade all the way to her hips. All she wore under that was a traditional pure white silk shift, and the breast-feeding bra under that, which under different circumstances would not be very sexy, but this bra was a dream, studded with precious jewels around the edges, made specifically for this occasion, specifically for her.

And Amir showed special appreciation for it.

She sighed his name as his lips found the clasp. Then he laid her gently on the bed, and the bra, along with the rest of her attire, was history.

Every ounce of focus she had left was needed to help him with his ceremonial robe and the rest of his clothes. It was like opening a Christmas present. Then his glorious body was finally bare and all hers to take.

His long fingers caressed her hips. Then moved lower. A delicious shiver zinged through her. Every part of her body responded to this man, had responded to him from the beginning.

He entered her in one long slide, claiming her lips in a searing kiss at the same time. She felt as if her nerve endings were exploding.

Nothing he did was rushed, as if he'd been planning this for a very long time. She ran her hands down his muscled back as desire burned through her. They rocked against each other, exquisitely slow at first, then building speed. A haze of sensual passion enveloped them, the tension growing, expanding, until together they flew into space.

Afterward, still twined together, her head on his shoulder, she looked at the flower-patterned ceiling, listened to the murmur of the celebrating crowd outside, the steady beat of Amir's heart in her ear.

She was a queen, the well-loved wife of Sheik Amir Khalid, her son his cherished heir, the hope of the country. Life was a thousand times stranger than fiction. She grinned against his warm skin.

This might not be how she had planned things when she'd first found out that she was pregnant, but she sure didn't mind the change.

"Remind me to run through a couple of things with you in the morning, before we leave for that honeymoon," he murmured into her hair, his voice thick with satisfaction and the need for sleep.

"Like what?"

"Not now."

"If you don't tell me now, I'll be up all night worrying that you want to buy me another palace or something." Receiving the keys on a velvet pillow had been quite a shock to her system at the end of the wedding ceremony.

He cracked open an eye.

"I didn't buy you a palace. The summer palace has been in my family for centuries."

"Fine. You *gave* it to me."

"Traditionally, it belongs to the queen."

"You know I don't like being given things." She was going to be teaching at the Royal University Medical School at the start of the next semester. Partially to encourage more women to enter the medical field, but also to make sure that she retained some of her independence, a plan that Amir wholeheartedly supported.

"Duly noted."

"So what?"

"So what what?"

"What do we need to talk about?"

He came up on an elbow and looked at her with a wary expression on his handsome face.

"I knew it! You *are* planning to give me something."

"All right. The supervisor of the royal nursery wants to know when to expect the second child. The finance minister wants to commission a picture of you for engraving on a set of commemorative silver coins he's issuing."

"Is that all?" She felt the blood drain from her face. She wasn't ready for the whole being-on-money-and-stamps thing.

"We'll have a ceremonial breakfast in the morning with the full court attending. You will be receiving my mother's jewels as your morning gift."

"Morning gift?" She hated how weak she sounded.

"The queen receives jewels from her husband the morning after the wedding night. Old tradition. Pay no mind to it."

She stared at him.

"Say something."

"Blazing buzzards."

A slow grin split his handsome face. "This is why I didn't want to tell you. Now you'll be up thinking and won't be able to sleep."

"That's for sure."

"There's only one thing to do." He drew his index finger slowly down the valley of her breasts.

Her skin tingled; her nipples puckered. "What?" She sounded a lot more breathless than she'd intended.

"I'm going to have to take your mind off all this," he said, then took her lips in a searing kiss.

Which felt just like what the doctor ordered. "There's a boatload on my mind, actually." She pulled her forehead into an exaggerated frown.

"That could mean that we'll be at this all night," he warned her and grinned.

* * * * *

&Harlequin®
INTRIGUE®

COMING NEXT MONTH

Available October 11, 2011

#1305 MAJOR NANNY
Daddy Corps
Paula Graves

#1306 ENGAGED WITH THE BOSS
Situation: Christmas
Elle James

#1307 CLASSIFIED
Colby Agency: Secrets
Debra Webb

#1308 STRANGER, SEDUCER, PROTECTOR
Shivers: Vieux Carré Captives
Joanna Wayne

#1309 WESTIN LEGACY
Open Sky Ranch
Alice Sharpe

#1310 BLACK OPS BODYGUARD
Donna Young

You can find more information on upcoming
Harlequin® titles, free excerpts and more at
www.HarlequinInsideRomance.com.

REQUEST YOUR FREE BOOKS!
2 FREE NOVELS PLUS 2 FREE GIFTS!

Harlequin®

INTRIGUE®

BREATHTAKING ROMANTIC SUSPENSE

YES! Please send me 2 FREE Harlequin Intrigue® novels and my 2 FREE gifts (gifts are worth about \$10). After receiving them, if I don't wish to receive any more books, I can return the shipping statement marked "cancel." If I don't cancel, I will receive 6 brand-new novels every month and be billed just \$4.49 per book in the U.S. or \$5.24 per book in Canada. That's a saving of at least 14% off the cover price! It's quite a bargain! Shipping and handling is just 50¢ per book in the U.S. and 75¢ per book in Canada.* I understand that accepting the 2 free books and gifts places me under no obligation to buy anything. I can always return a shipment and cancel at any time. Even if I never buy another book, the two free books and gifts are mine to keep forever.

182/382 HDN FEQ2

Name _____ (PLEASE PRINT)

Address _____ Apt. #

City _____ State/Prov. _____ Zip/Postal Code

Signature (if under 18, a parent or guardian must sign) _____

Mail to the **Reader Service:**
IN U.S.A.: P.O. Box 1867, Buffalo, NY 14240-1867
IN CANADA: P.O. Box 609, Fort Erie, Ontario L2A 5X3

Not valid for current subscribers to Harlequin Intrigue books.

**Are you a subscriber to Harlequin Intrigue books
and want to receive the larger-print edition?
Call 1-800-873-8635 or visit www.ReaderService.com.**

* Terms and prices subject to change without notice. Prices do not include applicable taxes. Sales tax applicable in N.Y. Canadian residents will be charged applicable taxes. Offer not valid in Quebec. This offer is limited to one order per household. All orders subject to credit approval. Credit or debit balances in a customer's account(s) may be offset by any other outstanding balance owed by or to the customer. Please allow 4 to 6 weeks for delivery. Offer available while quantities last.

Your Privacy—The Reader Service is committed to protecting your privacy. Our Privacy Policy is available online at www.ReaderService.com or upon request from the Reader Service.

We make a portion of our mailing list available to reputable third parties that offer products we believe may interest you. If you prefer that we not exchange your name with third parties, or if you wish to clarify or modify your communication preferences, please visit us at www.ReaderService.com/consumerschoice or write to us at Reader Service Preference Service, P.O. Box 9062, Buffalo, NY 14269. Include your complete name and address.

HI11B

Harlequin Romantic Suspense presents the latest book in the scorching new **KELLEY LEGACY** *miniseries from best-loved veteran series author Carla Cassidy*

Scandal is the name of the game as the Kelley family fights to preserve their legacy, their hearts…and their lives.

Read on for an excerpt from the fourth title
RANCHER UNDER COVER

Available October 2011
from Harlequin Romantic Suspense

"**W**ould you like a drink?" Caitlin asked as she walked to the minibar in the corner of the room. She felt as if she needed to chug a beer or two for courage.

"No, thanks. I'm not much of a drinking man," he replied.

She raised an eyebrow and looked at him curiously as she poured herself a glass of wine. "A ranch hand who doesn't enjoy a drink? I think maybe that's a first."

He smiled easily. "There was a six-month period in my life when I drank too much. I pulled myself out of the bottom of a bottle a little over seven years ago and I've never looked back."

"That's admirable, to know you have a problem and then fix it."

Those broad shoulders of his moved up and down in an easy shrug. "I don't know how admirable it was, all I knew at the time was that I had a choice to make between living and dying and I decided living was definitely more appealing."

She wanted to ask him what had happened preceding that six-month period that had plunged him into the bottom of the bottle, but she didn't want to know too much about him. Personal information might produce a false sense of intimacy that she didn't need, didn't want in her life.

"Please, sit down," she said, and gestured him to the table. She had never felt so on edge, so awkward in her life.

"After you," he replied.

She was aware of his gaze intensely focused on her as she rounded the table and sat in the chair, and she wanted to tell him to stop looking at her as if she were a delectable dessert he intended to savor later.

Watch Caitlin and Rhett's sensual saga unfold amidst the shocking, ripped-from-the-headlines drama of the Kelley Legacy miniseries in

RANCHER UNDER COVER

Available October 2011 only from Harlequin Romantic Suspense, wherever books are sold.

INTRIGUE